Nappy Head And All

Lynda Tidwell Morris

To Debi,
Happy reading.
It's been a pleasure
knowing you.
Lynda T. Morris

1/11

Outskirts Press, Inc.
Denver, Colorado

Chapter One

Mo'n used to say a woman's hair is her glory. I think she read that somewhere in the Bible. But I've found no glory in my hair. My hair brings me nothing but pain. All my life, I have been called black, ugly, and nappy head. It was by my own mama most of the time. Her name was Viola, but we called her Mo'n. Mo'n hated me. I didn't do any more wrong then the rest of my brothers and sisters; Isaiah, Samuel, Solomon, Ezekiel, Jeremiah, Esther, Sarah, or Big Sister -- but I, Nadine, got the most whippings and I didn't understand why. Mo'n didn't need a reason to beat me; she beat my ass just because it was Monday. She was my mama, but if she didn't want me, why didn't she just jump off our high porch and abort me? I would have been better off if she had because all babies go to heaven.

I realized at the young age of five that I had no voice in Mo'n and Daddy's house, so I spoke only when spoken too. My conversations were within myself, in my head -- but I wasn't crazy. I heard it was okay to talk to yourself as long as you didn't answer back.

Mo'n wouldn't even comb my hair. I admit I do have a bad grade of hair. It's what we called "barb wire" and "beat you back" because as soon as the straightening comb was pulled through it, the little nappy bee-bees rolled right back to the back of my neck.

Now Esther and Sarah had a good grade of hair like Mo'n, but Big Sister and I was cursed with Daddy's hair, I guess. Big Sister's hair wasn't as fine as Esther's and Sarah's, but she kept it nice. Mo'n made Big Sister comb my hair too and she didn't seem to mind. We called her Big Sister because she was the oldest of the children, but she wasn't big at all. Ola Mae, her real name, was all of five feet four inches tall, one hundred fifteen pounds soaking wet, dark smooth skin with a Coca-Cola bottle shaped body. She was very attractive. Daddy cussed out many Negroes for trying to talk to her. I didn't have her looks but I wanted a body like Ola Mae when I got older. I loved her a lot; maybe it was because Mo'n treated her bad too -- but she didn't beat her. She didn't like it when Mo'n beat me, and she stuck up for me if she was around when Mo'n did.

Five-O-Nine Redwood Avenue was where Daddy, Mo'n and the rest of us lived, in a wooden house that sat on the corner of Redwood and Fruitwood Streets. The wood was a rust color like that of worn railroad tracks. My Daddy worked on the railroads, and he helped build our house, which might explain the wood. Our house was built in 1938, twelve years before I was born. It had five small bedrooms, a modest-sized living room, a kitchen, and one bathroom that all eleven of us shared. Mo'n and Daddy shared a bedroom; the five boys one; Esther and Sarah shared a room, and Big Sister and I shared one. Sister and I probably shared a room because of the four girls, the two of us was dark-skinned. Mo'n was color struck, so I wouldn't put anything past her as to the reason; the two dark-skinned ones shared a room, and the two light-skinned ones shared a room. It was no secret that Esther, the second oldest, was Mo'n's favorite. Esther could do no wrong in Mo'n's eyes. If she had a fight with my other siblings, Mo'n always took her side. She was tall like Daddy, but she had Mo'n's mean ways and skin tone, the shade of black coffee with a lot of evaporated milk; I had Daddy's skin tone. Mo'n and Esther could have been sisters, because they were like two peas in a pod.

Our house was set high off the ground and had a lot of windows. The scariest thing about the house to me was the front steps. We had to climb fifteen steps to get to the front porch. When I was younger, I would hold on tight to the railing to climb up the steps and scoot down on my behind to go down them. Going down was much better than going up for sure. Several of my brothers and Esther knew how terrified I was of those steps and they threatened to push me down the steps so I would break my neck. Everything in me told me they meant it -- they were some low-down o' bastards. We had nice furniture in our living room and kitchen. Daddy brought it to the house after Grandma passed away and it looked good to me, but Mo'n didn't like it; she wanted new furniture. The kitchen furniture was really dining room furniture, but we didn't have a separate dining room like Grandma, so Daddy put the table and chairs in the kitchen and the china cabinet in the living room.

The house used electricity but we had a big, black, cast-iron potbelly stove to keep the house warm in the winter. It was supposed to heat the whole house, but it was in Mo'n and Daddy's room on the first floor. In the early morning before school, we all came downstairs and gathered around the stove to keep warm while Mo'n fixed breakfast. Sarah used to stand in front of the stove and when her dress got hot, she would jump back and say, "Hot diggity dog." Daddy told her over and over about saying that, but she just kept saying it. One morning, he gave her another warning and told her it was her last. She stopped that morning but the next morning, she did it again. Daddy must have known she would do it again because as soon as she started her ritual, he caught her by one arm and raised her up in the air and beat her with his bare hand: one lick for every word. "Didn't. I. Tell. You. To. Stop. That. Foolishness. When. I. Tell. You. To. Stop. That's. What. I. Mean. Do. You. Understand. Me?" That broke her and she never did it again. She never even stood near the stove again. Solomon and Ezekiel were the oldest, so they were responsible for keeping wood for the stove stockpiled on the back porch.

In the summertime we had a small air conditioner in the living room window, one of the many things Daddy's boss man, Mr. Turner, sold him when he had no more use for it; he told Daddy they were upgrading to central air and heat at his house. That air felt good, but Mo'n was not going to let us sit up in the living room all summer. She told us to get our behinds out the door and play somewhere while she sat up under the air conditioner. If we wanted to cool off from the Alabama heat, we went outside and sat under the big shade tree on the right side of the house. I don't know what kind of tree it was, but I called it a Hawaiian tree because of the all the leaves and the pretty pink flowers that blossomed on it. It was like the trees I saw in books about Hawaii. Sometimes, if Mo'n was in a good mood, she would let us turn on the hydrant with the water hose attached and we played in the water, but not before she hollered out the door to me, "Nadine, you better get in here and put a light bread sack on your head so it won't get wet. Your hair is nappy enough as it is."

Chapter Two

Daddy had been a preacher since I came out of Mo'n's womb. I had yet to hear him preach a sermon ... from the pulpit, anyway; but the fifth bedroom located downstairs, next to the pantry, in the kitchen was used as his study. There was a bed in the study for guests, too, but as far back as I can remember, we never had overnight guests; not even relatives. Mo'n's folks lived way out in the country and coming to visit us was like traveling to another state to them, so they never came. Daddy was an only child and Grandma and Grandpa were dead; they died before I was born. The bed was used quite regularly, though, when Daddy came home late, drunk from the bootlegger's house. He didn't like to sleep with Mo'n when he was drunk, so he slept in the study.

Daddy carried himself like he came from something. But if he did, we didn't benefit from it because he was tight with his money and didn't buy anything but necessities for the family and new clothes for himself. He never even talked about money until the weekend when he got a little liquor in his body; then he bragged about what his Daddy had. According to my Daddy, the Thomas family was one of the first Negro families in Opelika to own a vehicle: a black 1940 two-door Ford sedan.

Grandpa, God bless the dead, was an insurance man and sold

insurance to the black folks; he sold Mo'n's family insurance too. He was well-respected around town and the womenfolk admired the way he dressed. Daddy took after Grandpa when it came to dressing, they said.

Mo'n couldn't stand Daddy's folks because they didn't approve of their marriage. Daddy was eleven years older than Mo'n, and Grandpa and Grandma felt he married beneath him. I heard her tell Cousin Jessie Bell one day, when I slipped into the living room and sat on the floor by the low double windows that looked out to the porch and eavesdropped while they talked on the porch, that Grandpa wanted folks to believe that was his Ford, but the car really belonged to the insurance company he worked for. She said the Thomas family was some uppity niggers, but they didn't have a pot to piss in. I don't know what Grandpa and them had or didn't have, but Daddy had family photos of him taken when he was a baby. What black folks could afford portraits back then? Mo'n didn't have a picture to her name until after she married my Daddy. I don't know why she had such ill feelings for Daddy's folks, or why she still talked about them; they had been dead for years. But I knew one thing for sure: there was more to it than she was letting on. Something in the milk ain't clean, is what the old folks used to say.

Grandpa went to heaven before Grandma. One rainy evening, he was in a bad accident returning home after collecting insurance payments; he ran off into a ditch. They said the accident ain't what killed him, though. A fat man came along and while trying to help him out of the car, he fell on my Grandpa and smothered him. Grandma lived another seven years before she went on to see our Maker. Mo'n said to Cousin Jessie Bell, "If they had shit, we ain't seen none of it. All they left was that raggedy ass furniture that I don't want up in my house." There wasn't anything wrong with that furniture. I could tell it was of good quality and it was heavy, too. Mo'n might be the reason Daddy's folks didn't leave us anything. But if Grandpa and Grandma had left us something, Mo'n wouldn't know, because Daddy handled the money and issued her what she needed to pay insurance and make groceries.

Because Grandpa sold insurance, Daddy believed in buying insurance too. We had a dozen policies hanging along the hallway wall, each in its own vanilla envelope, like the one we used to bring home our school report cards in. The policies hung on the wall until Daddy paid them off, and then he would put them in a small, square, gray metal box under lock and key and dare anyone to touch the box. The insurance man came every Monday to collect. By the time Mo'n paid on all the policies, it would cost a whole dollar. One day Mo'n didn't want to pay the insurance man for one reason or another, so she told Isaiah to tell the insurance man she wasn't home. When Isaiah got to the door the man asked, "Is your mother home?"

Isaiah said, "No sir, she said she ain't here." The man smiled and told him to tell her he came by and left. Before the man could get down those fifteen steps, Isaiah shouted out to Mo'n, "Mo'n, he said he came by." I laughed so hard I about pissed in my panties. I was crying until Mo'n looked at me and asked what was funny.

"Nothing, Mo'n."

"It must be somethin' for you to laugh like that -- let me in on what's so funny, so I can laugh with you."

She knew why the hell I was laughing, so why was she asking me why I was laughing? She was dead set on getting an answer out of me, and I was dead set on saying nothing.

"Nothing, huh? You're a lie. What I done told you about lying?" *You talking to me about lying when you lied when you told Isaiah to lie and tell the insurance man you weren't home.* I got quiet because I knew I was damned if I told her and damned if I didn't. "You hear me talking to you, Nadine? You gonna stand your black, nappy head ass there and act dumb?" She thumped Isaiah on the head. "Boy, take your black ass outside somewhere and play." She then pointed at me. "Go get me a switch -- I'm gonna give you something to laugh about." I had to go outside and pick the switch she would beat me with. The first time I ever picked a switch, I got the smallest limb I could find and when Mo'n beat me, it never broke; it just bent. Isaiah told me later that when I had to get a switch, I should get a big one because it would break faster. I learned two lessons that day: big switches break faster, and not to laugh about anything that went on in that house.

Sunday mornings Daddy always got up early and put on his "Sunday go to meeting" clothes, ready to go to the house of the Lord. Every Sunday God sent, as soon as we opened the door and stepped into the vestibule, Daddy would say, "Fix yourself up 'fore we go in." I hated that ritual; we weren't wearing anything to fix up. Mo'n would inspect his clothes to make sure he was fit to be seen and then straighten the duster dress she was wearing. Daddy was dressed in one of his many suits. He was wearing a black suit with fine gray pinstripes; a white long-sleeved shirt with gold cuff links that his father left him; a red tie with a red and white hankie hanging over the left breast pocket; black and gray pinstripe socks; a pair of black and white wing-tip shoes; and a black-brimmed hat with a gray satin band wrapped around it. He didn't wear the hat in the church because it was disrespectful for men to wear hats in the Lord's house. He placed it on top of his black leather Bible like it was a trophy.

Yes, my Daddy was sharp while the rest of us, including Mo'n, looked like shit. He took pride in his clothes and so did Mo'n. We had a big heavy duty washing machine with two rollers on the top to wring the clothes, sitting on the back porch, but Mo'n used a washboard and round tin tubs to hand wash Daddy's clothes. She washed his clothes in sweet soap, hung them on the line, and used two long wood planks to prop up the line so Daddy's clothes wouldn't sag to the ground.

As we entered into the sanctuary, we marched single file from the tallest to the shortest child, with Daddy leading the way and Mo'n coming up the rear. Daddy stopped at the pews he wanted us to sit on and after we were situated, he made his way up to the pulpit where he sat in the high back chair to the right of Pastor Dixon's chair. He sat down and crossed his long legs, looking dignified, observing the congregation until Pastor Dixon got whined up. Daddy then became Pastor Dixon's cheerleader. He shouted, *"Amen! Preach, doc! Well, and yes sir,"* louder than the choir singing my favorite song, "I'd Fly Away."

"Some glad morning when this life is over, I'll fly away… I'd fly away old glory, I'd fly away. When I die hallelujah bye and bye, I'd fly away." I've always liked that song. The first time I heard the choir sing it, I couldn't keep my seat. With all I went through with Mo'n, I was hoping that I would stand up and fly away, but at the end of the song, I was still there, only sitting. I came to understand the flying away would come by and by. But the song would overtake me and before I knew it, I would be up with lifted hands toward heaven shouting, "Yes Lord! Yes Lord!" In our church, shouting meant you had caught the spirit and it was the sanctuary police's duty to help you release it. Mo'n said it was the devilment I got into. Two ushers, dressed in black double-breasted dresses with white cuffs on quarter sleeves, white gloves, and white, old but freshly polished, laced shoes, would rush over to me and take hold of both my arms. They pushed me down in the pew and fanned me with hand fans that had Dr. King's face on the front side and Holmes and Jackson Funeral Home information on the back. We didn't have air conditioning in the church and during the summer it was some kind of hot in there. So since the sanctuary police wanted to fan me -- *Fan me*! I caught the spirit on a regular basis.

The choir always did a wonderful job rendering songs for worship service, but Esther always had something negative to say about the choir. She criticized how they sounded, how they clapped, and how they moved in unison from side and side. She would comment about what she would do if she was a member of the choir, which would never happen as long as Daddy was alive and well. That heifer could sing; she had been in the school choir, she sang around the house, and sometimes she sang while she combed my hair, between the licks to my head. She thought she sounded like Mahalia Jackson, and she did, but she was so conceited when it came to her singing. Daddy didn't like that about her. She begged him to let her join the choir and he said no. She got particular one day and asked him why she couldn't sing for the Lord. He told her she only wanted to sing to show off and that when you sing for the Lord it ain't for form or fashion. Daddy was right -- that was the reason she wanted to join the choir, but I wished she was a member; maybe then she wouldn't have been so mean and low-down. When Daddy wouldn't let her sing the gospel in the choir, all she sung when Daddy wasn't around was the blues, and Mo'n wouldn't say a word.

When all the shouters were calmed down, Pastor Dixon stood up and walked to the podium wearing his black crepe preacher's robe with two big gold crosses embroidered on the front. He stood as if he was Moses on the mount and proclaimed, "The Lord is in

His holy temple, let all the earth keep silent..." Now he had been enjoying the singing too; he had stomped his feet and did his Indian dance, but after the proclamation he got serious. Like a fortuneteller, he looked fiercely around the room as if he could tell what kind of hellish life we had lived on last week. *Lord, I know you know all things, but I can't see You looking at me right now -- but Pastor Dixon is. So, Lord, when Pastor Dixon's eyes reach me, please don't let him see what I did last week.* When he finished scanning the congregation, he read two Scriptures and closed his Bible. Not everybody in the church had a Bible, but Daddy had one even though I'd never seen him open it to find the text. If the truth be told, I don't think Daddy could any more read than a man on the moon. Mo'n talked a lot of shit when she talked to Cousin Jessie Bell, but at home, she read to Daddy -- one of her many submissive duties. Pastor Dixon would preach a whole sermon from those two Scriptures and he didn't have to open his Bible again; he had everything he wanted to say on a piece of white, ruled, three-hole notebook paper. I enjoyed all his sermons except the one on fornication. I used to like that one too until I got older and understood what fornication meant. I didn't want him to preach on that because it made me uncomfortable.

When we weren't at our home church, we visited other churches, and I hated that for two reasons. First, we walked everywhere we went because there wasn't a car big enough to carry all eleven of us at the same time; and second, Daddy was known to invite other preachers over for dinner when we visited other churches. Mo'n always cooked a feast for Sunday dinner while she fixed breakfast, so she could relax after service. She would cook fried chicken, fried fatback meat, sweetbread, crackling cornbread, collard greens with ham hocks, fried green tomatoes, fried squash, field peas with okra, and my favorite, apple pie. The cinnamon and nutmeg aroma drifted through the air from the apple pie Mo'n had baked, and it made me want to eat dessert for breakfast.

We always looked forward to Sunday dinner so we could eat the vegetables Daddy brought from the "Watermelon Man" when he came through our neighborhood on Saturday mornings. The man drove an 1955 beat-up blue Ford truck up the street with his head out the window as if he couldn't see through the windshield, hollering, "Watermelons, watermelons; I got field peas, butterbeans, okra, tomatoes, collard greens and mustards." He came down from Chamber County. When the truck came to a stop, an old grubby man got out of his truck, puffing a hand-rolled Prince Albert tobacco cigarette. "It's fresh, me and my boys got up 'fore day this morning and picked it."

As he and my Daddy talked, he told Daddy he used cow manure to fertilize and grow his garden. When the other neighbors saw the truck, they all started coming off their porches and out of the houses to meet the truck. We children would sit on the porch while the other children from the neighborhood ran out and climbed up on the truck. We wanted to run to the truck, too -- or I did, but I knew better than to go unless Daddy beckoned for me to come. He knew I liked picking the watermelons; he had showed me how to thump them to hear how they sounded. The sound of the watermelon determined if it was ripe enough to eat; Daddy called me off the porch to pick three. Daddy would buy watermelons, and bushels of field peas, collard greens, squash, and okra for us, and called for the boys to come out to the truck and carry it all back to the house. We looked at all the vegetables and knew what we all would be doing for the next two hours: sitting on the front porch shelling peas, cleaning and cutting collard greens, and slicing squash and okra. As soon as Daddy walked into the house, Solomon and Ezekiel started cracking jokes about how some greedy preachers were going to reap the benefit of our labor. They low-rated all bootleg preachers. If Daddy or Mo'n heard some of the words that came out of their mouths, they would have sent them out in the woods to tarry for days after they finished skinning them alive.

Sure enough, when Sunday came, three big-neck preachers showed up for dinner. That meant neither Mo'n nor we would be allowed to eat until they were finished eating. Mo'n waited on them hand and foot; she was tired but she just grinned and bore it. Daddy treated Mo'n like she was his housemaid. Honestly, Mo'n did carry herself like one. She was a little plump; weight gained after giving birth to all of us over the years. I've seen pictures of Mo'n when she first married Daddy, and she wasn't always plump. I could see why Daddy wanted her back then. She was much younger than him, had curves in all the right places like Ola Mae, and was well-groomed. Any man would have wanted her on his arm. I heard Mo'n tell Cousin Jessie Bell about the time a man was outside the church selling stockings while she and Daddy were walking into the church. The man stopped Daddy and asked him if he wanted to buy his daughter some stockings and Daddy cussed the man out and told him Mo'n wasn't his daughter, she was his wife. Mo'n thought that was so funny but she didn't laugh about it around Daddy. She used to keep her hair nice; now she kept her head covered during the week with head rags and wore big, loose duster dresses every day, trying to hide the extra pounds she had put on over the years. On Sundays she replaced the head rags with hats, but she still dressed in second-hand clothes like the rest of us. I guess Daddy didn't find her eye-catching anymore. From as long as I could remember, he always talked to Mo'n like she was one of us children. He would wait until the other preachers were there at the house and ask Mo'n to rub his feet, and she did it.

Daddy always said, "Remember the Sabbath Day and keep it holy. You ain't supposed to work on the Sabbath, that's God day." He didn't even allow us to iron on Sunday morning; if we didn't iron our clothes on Saturday, we had to wear them to church on Sunday wrinkled. But that law didn't apply to us or Mo'n when it came to impressing his fellow brothers of the cloth. Isaiah, Samuel, and Jeremiah's job was to fan the flies while those bastards sat there and ate all the good pieces of chicken. Daddy didn't let us girls come near the dinner table while they were there because he didn't want us around menfolks. When they were done, all we had were a couple of chicken necks and backs to split between us. It's true. Baptist preachers like chicken, but they also like anything else their greedy asses can get hold of. After they finished eating they left and went home to eat again, and we were hungry. Mo'n was fit to be tied at Daddy, but she never said a word to him about it. And he did it time and time again. At least we could look forward to our Sunday evening watermelon treat.

Chapter Three

Everything was segregated in the late fifties, and except for a few juke joints and hole in the wall clubs that had one way in and one way out, there wasn't much for the black folks to do. For so long, Daddy had shielded us from the prejudice and hatred he experienced on a daily basis. Our entertainment was going to church or sitting around the living room listening to the evening news on the little brown AM radio that Mr. Turner sold to Daddy. One night after the news, the "Amos and Andy" show came on and two white men were on the radio acting as if they were black men. As we listened, everybody cracked up laughing; me too, inwardly. It angered Daddy and in the midst of us laughing, he jumped up and turned the radio off. He told us there was nothing funny about two white men entertaining white folks by portraying the black man as stupid and lazy. He said the white man was always putting the black man down, but if the truth be told, the black man worked two times harder than the white man for half the pay. It was just a funny show on the radio to us, but after Daddy explained how degrading it was and what was really going on, we understood his anger.

Daddy was constantly disrespected by a few of the white men on his job, but he stood his ground. Mr. Henry, the only other black man on the job, didn't, and it frustrated Daddy. Daddy told Mo'n when he would tell Mr. Henry to stand up for himself; his response would be, "I got mouths to feed; it ain't nothing I can do. I'm on these white folk jobs." It was no secret Daddy didn't trust white men. He said he didn't trust them any further than he could throw them. That's why I never understood why he hung the blond-haired, blue-eyed Jesus up in an 11 by 14 black frame. That was not the image of the Jesus I believed in or read about in his Bible. My Jesus had hair like wool, eyes as a flame of fire, feet like fine brass as if they burned in a furnace, and a voice as the sound of many waters. I identified with this Jesus' hair and skin, not the frail Jesus Daddy hung on the living room wall, right next to the picture of the Reverend Doctor Martin Luther King, Jr. Daddy didn't know about my Jesus and I never heard Pastor Dixon describe Him like that; maybe it was because he never preached from the book of Revelation. Maybe he hadn't got that far in the Bible yet; it was the last book in the Bible.

"Y'all get on up and go get yourself ready for bed. You got school in the morning."

It was zero dark thirty in the morning when Mo'n woke Big Sister and me up so she could comb my nappy hair for school. Big Sister didn't go to school, but she got up anyway to comb my hair, especially when Mo'n threatened to drag her out of the bed on her head. She had got to where she stayed out later, but Mo'n didn't know about it. If she had known Sister had just got home two hours before she woke her up to comb my hair, she would have wrung her neck. On those mornings, Mo'n would come in and say to Sister, "If I have to come in here and tell you to get up one more time, you gonna wish you had got up the first time -- your black ass been sleeping too damn much anyway." Big Sister would drag herself up, even though she was sleepy, to comb my hair. She never mistreated me like Esther.

We all walked to school together; only blacks went to our school. The white folks had their own school in the white folks' section of town. They said the white children got the best of everything at their school and we got their leftovers, like something was wrong with that. Pastor Dixon always preached you should be thankful for what you got. Listening to them complain, you would think things were supposed to be different than they were. Isaiah and I were in the same homeroom. The girls said Isaiah was the cute twin and I was the ugly one. Several of them came up to me one day and asked why my twin was so much prettier than me. I had an answer for them that day -- I told them we were both fourteen, but we were not twins. Then they wanted to know how that happened, like I was supposed to know. If I had to guess, I reckon as soon as Mo'n dropped one child, she was pregnant with another one. There were nine of us, and it was rumored that Daddy got three more somewhere else before he married Mo'n, but I did not believe that.

The children at school said I talked proper like the white folks. I don't know how they came to that conclusion; I lived in the house with black folks that didn't talk proper at all. I guess it was all the reading I did. I spent a lot of time reading from Daddy's Bible and the black folks' magazine, *Ebony*, which I got from my teacher, Ms. Harris. It was good to pick up a book and see nothing but black folks in it doing good for themselves. Ms. Harris kept the magazines on the corner of her desk and I asked if I could read them when she was finished with them, and she started giving them to me when she was done.

Isaiah was a star on the football team and was popular at school, but I was the smart one. He had lots of friends; boys and girls. Me, nobody even noticed me unless I was with Isaiah, but I was thankful for that little bit of attention. Any other time when I walked the school halls those same children would walk right by me like I was invisible. If only I was invisible or had the ability to disappear -- I would go to that heaven Pastor Dixon preached about, where the streets are paved with gold, way up yonder in the clouds. That sounded like the place to be, and I would make just one request to God, that Mo'n and Esther didn't show up there. It's okay for Big Sister, Sarah, Daddy, and the boys, but seeing those two would ruin it for me. But then according to Pastor Dixon and the Bible, if you don't go to heaven you going to hell -- so I shouldn't be like that. Okay Lord, let them in; just give me a little time to myself before they get there.

Another thing, when I get to heaven, I want to ask God why He said in the Bible, "Spare the rod, spoil the child," because when it came to me, Mo'n lived by that Scripture, but only where I was concerned. I can count on one hand how many times Isaiah got a beating, and it was nothing like how Mo'n beat me. Her intent was to cause me as much pain as she could. I believe Mo'n looked for a reason to beat me. The severe beatings started when I was five. Every time she beat me, she made me take off all my clothes so she could beat me naked. She used every bit of strength in her body with each lick, and all I could do was stand there in pain until she got tired. I knew better than to run. She had warned me that if I ever ran from her, she would beat me for old and new and she meant it. When she finished, blood ran from the many welts she left all over my body. When she finished, she would tell me to put my clothes back on and stop crying before she gave me something to cry about.

The other day as we walked home from school, I ran ahead and when I got to the house, Cousin Jessie Bell was sitting on the porch with Mo'n. I think she was Mo'n's cousin for real. She lived two houses down and she and Mo'n normally hollered back and forth across the yard to talk, but she was on Mo'n's porch today, so she must have had some gossip. I wished I could turn invisible until I got past them because I knew that just as soon as I stepped one foot on that porch, Mo'n was going to need something.

"Good afternoon," I said.

"Hey baby, how you doing," was Cousin Jessie Bell's response.

With no greeting, Mo'n looked at me and said, "Fetch me a glass of ice water." *Get it your damn self, what would you have done if I had not come home?* Mo'n turned to Cousin Jessie Bell and said, "All I can offer you is a glass of water."

Jessie Bell looked at me and said "Yeah baby, get me a glass if you don't mind."

"Yes ma'am."

I went on in, put my books down, went and opened the refrigerator. Mo'n could have offered her something else to drink; we had drinks -- lemonade and iced tea -- in the refrigerator, but they were for Daddy. Mo'n listened for the refrigerator door to open and close and when I held it open three seconds too long, she opened the screen door and hollered, "Nadine, stop holding that ice box open, gal, running up that electric bill! Get the water and shut it up!"

If I had been up to an ass whipping that day, I would have gone and told Mo'n she had other stuff to drink in the refrigerator in front of Cousin Jessie Bell. If she wasn't my momma, I would have spit in her water. When I had poured the water, I decided to walk lightly back out to the porch so I could hear what they was talking about. Cousin Jessie Bell was talking about Ms. Lillie Pearl. Ms. Lillie Pearl lived in a small, square, yellow house on a dirt road just around the street from our house. The road didn't have a name, but she lived on the same dirt road a juke joint called Ballerina Inn was on. She sold candy and ice cream. Her husband died a few years earlier and she lived alone. Ms. Lillie Pearl didn't bother anybody; she just planted hundreds of plastic pastel flowers all over her yard and even put some in her hedge bushes. She loved flowers and because they were plastic, she could enjoy them 365 days a year. She loved them so much she even wore them on her person every day the Lord sent, just like Ms. Magdalene loved the color purple and wore it every day.

I didn't know how Ms. Lillie Pearl came to love flowers, but Ms. Magdalene said purple was royalty. She thought it made her more spiritual, too, and the reason I knew this was because I made the mistake of asking her one day why she wore purple every day and straight away she was quicken, caught up in the Holy Ghost and started speaking some crazy shit. She was so full of the spirit that all I could make out from her was its royalty. She wanted me to believe that she was drunk in the spirit, but I saw the bottle of white lightning sticking out of her purple housecoat. She was one of the bootleggers whose house Daddy frequented, aside from the fact that she rarely even went to church. She must have thought just because she sent "send by money" by Daddy, she was on her way to heaven anyhow.

Ms. Lillie Pearl, she didn't go to church either, but she was one of the nicest ladies I knew. So what in hell could Cousin Jessie Bell say about her? She needed to worry about her own business, because her husband, Mr. Arthur Lee, was doing it with Ms. Vernell, the neighborhood drunk. Two Fridays earlier, he and Ms. Vernell were on the side of his house, right next to Cousin Jessie Bell's bedroom window, and she didn't even know it. Why? Because she was too damn busy sticking her nose in other folks' business.

Chapter Four

We had just got home from school when from the bottom of the steps we heard Daddy cursing and saying words I'd never heard him say before. I was already passive and scared of everything, so I could not bring myself to climb the steps and go in the house. The other children went on up the steps and into the house, but I sat on the bottom step and listened. Daddy's rage stopped long enough for the children to pass through the living room, and then it started up again. It had something to do with Big Sister getting knocked up. I think that meant she was pregnant. Daddy was telling Mo'n that Big Sister had to go.

"Lord a' mercy R. L. -- where the gal going? She ain't got nowhere to go!"

"She ain't bringing another young'n in here -- I don't care where she gwine, but she gotta get the hell outta my house, and I mean that thing."

He quoted something from the Bible. I know he didn't read, so he must have memorized it from hearing someone else say it. Mo'n didn't even stick up for Sister, she just told her she had to go. What kind of mama would allow Daddy to just throw her child out in the street with nowhere to go? Around our house, what he said was gospel and under his roof he was the head Negro in charge. He didn't do a lot of beating; his look put the fear of God in us. When Sister walked down the steps to where I was, crying, I asked her what I was going to do without her, and who was going to comb my nappy hair. I wanted to know where she was going, and she said she didn't know, but as soon as she got settled, she would come back and visit me. I put my arms around her neck and clasped my fingers together so I could hold on to her for as long as I could. I didn't want her to leave me; I loved her.

She hugged me back until Daddy walked out on to the porch and looked down at us. "Nadine, get on in this here house, wash your face, and cut out all that noise. Come on now -- don't make me come down there and get you!" I heard Daddy but I just couldn't let go of Sister. Looking up at Daddy, Big Sister tried to break loose, telling me she had to go. She tried to separate my fingers so she could take my arms from around her neck, but I wouldn't let go. Mo'n came out of the house and walked down the steps and snatched my fingers loose. Big Sister walked up the street carrying the pillowcase that held all her belongings. That had to be the saddest day of my life -- even Mo'n felt sorry for me that day. She wiped the snot and tears from my face with an apron she had hand-sewn using an old flower printed sheet. She went in the pocket of the apron, handed me a nickel, and told me to walk around to Ms. Lillie Pearl and buy myself an ice cream cone. I was happy for the money to buy the cone, but I wanted Big Sister more. I stood at the edge of the yard and watched her as she walked up the street alone; she never looked back. How could Daddy and Mo'n just throw their child out in the street like that? Everything in me wanted to run after her and Mo'n knew it.

I didn't hear Mo'n call me because I was fixed on Big Sister walking up the street. "Nadine, Nadine!" I jumped. "Go on round to Lillie Pearl, and get on back to this house." As I walked, I kept looking back at Big Sister until I turned the corner to Ms. Lillie Pearl and could no longer see her. I thought about how much harder it would be on me with her gone. All the way to Ms. Lillie Pearl's house I kept saying, "Lord have mercy on my poor soul." I said it all the way to Ms. Lillie Pearl's doorstep. I didn't realize she was sitting on the porch when I reached her house and she heard me pleading to the Lord.

"Baby, what's wrong?"

I told her Big Sister was gone and that I would not see her again. Ms. Lillie Pearl asked where she had gone and I told her I didn't know, but she said she would come back and visit when she got settled. I started to cry again something awful. You would have thought somebody died, and that's what it felt like to me. Ms. Lillie Pearl told me she believed Sister would come back if she said she would and I should not worry my head about it. It wasn't just my head I was worrying about; it was my ass when Mo'n got through with it. So I had something to worry about. Only my Daddy could save me from Mo'n, and he worked during the day.

"Bless your heart -- sit right there, baby, and let Ms. Lillie Pearl go fix you a cone." She came back with three big scoops of the three favors: strawberry, vanilla, and chocolate. She knew those were the flavors I liked, and she didn't even charge me. She told me to keep my nickel for the next time. Ms. Lillie Pearl was so nice to me; I wished at least ten times that she was my mama instead of Mo'n. I'd take her any day, with her plastic flowers obsession and all.

With Big Sister gone, Mo'n made Esther comb my hair. Esther despised combing my hair and she made sure I knew it. She knew I was tender headed but she didn't care. She swore my hair hurt her hands when she combed it and she handled my head like it was a rag doll; snatching and pulling and plaiting it as tight as she could. Every time she finished combing my hair, I had fine, swollen bumps around every plait on my head, and it would hurt so bad. When I couldn't take it no more, I would put my hand on top of my head to try and protect it, and Esther would beat my hand with the comb until I put my hand down.

I cried so, and all Mo'n said was, "Shut up, you act like somebody trying to kill your black, nappy head ass." I was surprised I still had my right mind after Esther finished combing my hair. Mo'n always told me I didn't have the sense God gave a billy goat. *I'm smarter than any of your other children*, I thought. I was thankful when Big Sister was home, but she had been gone for a year with no word. I knew she got wherever she ended up and forgot all about me. But I understood, because when I could leave this house I would, and forget it too. At least now Sister didn't have to follow Daddy around on the weekend or put up with Mo'n cussing her out all the time with her religious ass.

In early spring, Mo'n had all of us, except Esther, out in our garden pulling weeds. Daddy planted okra, tomatoes, and peppers in the garden. While out there one day, I got so thirsty I ran to the water hydrant attached to the side of the house and the knob was broken. I was not able to turn it on, so I ran back to the back of the house, up the back steps, opened the screen door, and ran straight to the refrigerator and opened it just as Mo'n walked in. Lord, why did I do that?

"I know you didn't just bring your dirty, nappy head, black ass from out that door and open my damn ice box."

There was no need to explain to her that I was thirsty; she would have said I was talking back, so I just said, "Yes ma'am." I was overdue for an ass whipping by two days anyway. I saw the way she rolled her eyes at me when Daddy brought a grape sucker home on Saturday afternoon and gave it to me. I enjoyed that sucker that day, because I knew what the consequences would be for me because he gave me the sucker -- a Southern ass whipping at her first opportunity. The phone rang and she had to answer it. It was probably Cousin Jessie Bell. That was the only person who called her. If they weren't hollering across the yard or sitting on the front porch, they talked on the telephone. She was Mo'n's only friend.

I followed her into the living room and she turned and said, "You stand right there and don't you move. I'm gonna fix you for going in my damn ice box with your dirty hands when I answer this phone." As she walked over to the phone, Esther was running from the back to answer it too. She was too good to be outside pulling weeds like the rest of us. Mo'n reached the phone before Esther and suddenly, she wanted to take the call in her bedroom.

"Hold on a minute -- let me get to the phone in my bedroom."

"Mo'n, I'd hang it up for you."

"With those dirty hands? Esther, hang this here phone up when I get to the one in my bedroom."

She hollered out for Esther to hang up, and Esther pressed the button and released it like she had hung it up, but she never put the handset back on the base. She was eavesdropping on Mo'n's phone call, but I was not going to tell Mo'n, because Esther had to comb my hair -- and besides that, she would have figured out a way to turn it on me. She stood there listening and when Daddy walked in from work, she eased the phone down and spoke to Daddy.

"Good evening."

"Hey Daddy."

"What you doing standing there with that black dirt on your hands? Get in there and wash your hands."

"Mo'n told me not to move until she gets off the phone."

"Get in there and wash your hands, gal." *Thank you Daddy! Thank you Daddy! Thank you Daddy!* He saved me that day. When Mo'n heard his voice, she called for him. When I came out of the bathroom, the door to Mo'n and Daddy's bedroom was closed, but I could hear Daddy's voice coming through the door. I don't know who he was talking to, but he was furious. He said, "If you even try, I will find you and kill you. You better not ever call my house with this foolishness again, you hear me!"

Who in the world was Daddy talking to, and why in the world would he want to kill them? He sounded convincing, but my Daddy wouldn't kill anybody; he was a man of the cloth. But somebody had made him mad. When Mo'n and Daddy opened the door and came out of their bedroom, they were acting normal. They didn't act like Daddy had just finished cussing somebody out. I was sitting on the sofa when Mo'n spoke to me in a calm voice. "I see you washed your dirty hands." I didn't say anything. "Now, get on in there and get you some water, and don't you ever go in that ice box with dirty hands. Do you understand me?"

"Yes, ma'am." *I'm not thirsty now!* I had drunk water from the bathroom sink, but I went on in the kitchen and got the water.

Springtime was my favorite time of year. I got to take off my heavy coat and put on the navy blue sweater with the white anchor embroidered on the upper left side. Mo'n got it at the thrift store and I wore it with everything. In the springtime, there was something splendid about seeing nature wake up from its long nap. The trees and flowers came alive again and dispersed beautiful fragrances in the fresh air. The bumblebees, June bugs, and butterflies begin to return from wherever they go during the winter months. I had yet to catch a butterfly; they say if you catch one, bite its head off, and run around the house three times, you will get a new dress. I would have loved a new dress, but I much preferred seeing the butterflies fly around with their heads on. Not only was the air fresher, the days seemed to be much longer and brighter. If I could, I would sleep outside this time of the year.

When I was younger I used to follow Isaiah and some of the neighborhood boys down to the brook that separated the Washingtons' land from our land. When I got used to going, I would sometimes go there alone to get out of Mo'n's way. The water in that brook was so cold, and we would drink from it. Isaiah showed me how to cup my hands and told me I had to drink the water that continued to run downstream because it was good water. I didn't understand the reason for that, but I did what he said and the water was good even though there were weeds and sticks and some of everything else in it. We went to the brook to search for crawfish to keep for pets. We kept them out of the water and when they died, we would have a funeral for them in the back yard. The congregation would sit on the back steps and Isaiah would be the preacher. He impersonated Pastor Dixon and I would be his cheerleader just like Daddy was to Pastor Dixon when he preached. One of Cousin Jessie Bell's nephews was up to visit one summer from Louisiana and he said back in Louisiana, they ate crawfish. We told that boy he was crazy.

When we got older and stopped going to the brook, if I needed to get away from Mo'n, I found a safe haven in the window, in the bedroom the five boys shared. They were always out somewhere, so I could sit in there, take off my top, and nurse the welts Mo'n left all over my body. There I had out of body experiences; the next best thing since I couldn't just lie down and die. One day after one of my beatings, I went to the boys' room, pulled the curtain back and stared out the window, day dreaming about the day I get out of Mo'n and Daddy's house. This one day in particular, I pulled back the curtains and saw the light-skinned boy that lived right behind us. He looked like a black Indian with thick, wavy, black hair. His Daddy look like an Indian too, but his mama was black as smut. What did his Daddy see in her? She was black as me and kept her hair pulled back and twisted in a bun. She came out on their front porch and called the black Indian to her and gave him a big hug for some reason. Seeing that gave me butterflies and I closed my eyes tight and imagined that it was me getting the hug. Oh, the feeling I felt in the pit of my stomach! I didn't want to open my eyes because it felt so good. I never knew a hug could feel so good. The only hug I ever received was from Sister, the day she left which was a sad day for me. As I sit there taking it all in, I felt as if I was being watched, so I opened my eyes and found that boy looking up at me; I closed those curtains fast. What if he saw my titties? He wouldn't see much; two bumps that looked like mosquito bites.

I overheard some of the girls talking at school, and they said if you wanted your titties to grow, boys have to feel on them, and that wasn't going to happen to me. I figured I would probably be an old maid before I got married, or no one would marry me because I was black and my hair was nappy. Out of curiosity, I pulled the curtains back to see if he was still there and he was, looking up at me, motioning for me to come down. He must be a fool -- if Mo'n even knew I was sitting in that window with no top on, that would be the last time I sat in any window. I put my top on and left the room. It would be years before I actually met the black Indian boy.

Chapter Five

Today at school, my stomach was bothering me. I felt pain I have never felt before and I asked the Lord what was happening because I had never felt that kind of pain before. I went to the school front office and they didn't give a damn about me because they didn't know my folks. Rhonda Morgan, a light- skinned girl with hair down her back, was in there with a stomachache too. She thought she was something because she had "good hair" and it was long. Ms. Brown, the secretary, babied her ass. "Rhonda, honey do you want me to call your mother? Do you need her to pick you up?"

Rhonda's parents were one of the few black families with a business in Opelika. Cousin Jessie Bell said Rhonda's granddaddy was a white man and that's how her daddy came to own a filling station. There probably was some truth to that because he did look mixed, which would explain Rhonda's long hair, because her mama's hair wasn't long at all. Her mama wore a long, red, white woman wig that looked like the hair on the big, tall plastic dolls I saw in the Top Dollar Store window. But I'm not going to lie -- if I had a choice between the wig she wore and the hair on my head, I would take the wig; in black.

Ms. Brown looked at me and said, "Do you want a Bayer aspirin or BC powder? Because you need to get back to class." *Forget you, skank -- I know I've got to go back to class. I don't have a way home, no way.* We did eventually get a car but Daddy was at work and we knew not to cost him to have to take time off from work. If we did, we had better be one foot in the grave. But if I had a way, I wouldn't go; Mo'n was there.

"BC, ma'am." Rhonda was sitting there with a glass of water in her hand, and Ms. Brown gave me the BC powder and told me to use the water fountain outside the office. I took the BC and walked out the office and over to the water fountain. I placed the powder on my tongue and took a few sips of water from the fountain and walked back to my class. Over time, the pain eased but I felt miserable all day and the rain coming down outside my classroom window didn't help. I had hoped it would stop before school let out, but no such luck; we had to walk home in the pouring rain. We were soaked when we got there and when we climbed those steps Mo'n met us at the door.

"Wipe your feet off and get on in there and get out them there wet clothes." Mo'n looked me over and said, "Nadine you done became a woman -- get on in there and clean yourself up." I wondered how she came to that conclusion just by looking at me soaking wet. *So I'm a damn woman because I walked home in the pouring rain and cold -- or because my nipples are showing through this wet blouse?* It must have been the look on my face, because Mo'n pointed to my socks, and when I looked down they were stained with blood.

"Oh my God, Mo'n, I'm bleeding!" I had no clue where it came from until I saw it mixed with rain trickling down my leg from under my skirt and onto my socks. I looked up at Mo'n in shock.

"Get on in there and clean up, gal." I walked to the back and Mo'n followed me with a worn sheet. She tore it into pieces, folded it and told me to put it in my panties. She told me that I needed to change it when it got full and wrap the used rag up and put it in a brown grocery bag before I put it in the garbage. She gave me so many instructions that day; I was in a daze but I remember one thing she said very plain. She said, "You a woman now and you can have churin but you better keep your damn legs closed cause ain't no churin coming in this here house. You hear me?"

I nodded my head, still in shock about blood coming from my body when I hadn't cut myself. I don't remember her talking to my other sisters about having children. My other sisters had to bleed, but I don't remember -- maybe it just happened to me. But at that moment, I didn't remember much of anything. But then Sister was knocked up when she left, so she had to bleed. Children were the last thing on my mind and I hoped becoming a woman didn't mean I would be bleeding the rest of my life; damn having children. They can stay in the log they come from.

When Daddy got home, Mo'n told him I was on the rag and he too said I was a woman now. I didn't know what to call the bleeding at the time, so I named it the red baron. After three days of changing rags the bleeding stopped. That was a happy day but it didn't take me long to find out that was not the end, because from that month forward I got stomachaches that warn the red baron was on the way. That shit was too much for a child to bear -- I see now why they say you're a woman. When the pain got too bad, Mo'n boiled water and put it in a big red water bag and placed it on my stomach; it eased the pain a lot when she did that for me, and I almost felt she loved me a little. Another good thing that came out of having the red baron -- Mo'n didn't beat me when I was on the rag, and because I had become a woman, she stopped making me take off all my clothes when she did beat me.

Chapter Six

Christmas 1962, Daddy got us our first "black and white" television. His boss man sold it to him for fifteen dollars. He was getting a color one for his family and told Daddy if he wanted the old set, he could give him a couple of dollars each payday until he paid it off. He gave him the outside antenna to go with the television for free. Daddy attached it outside the living room window. We thought we were rich because we had our own picture show in our living room. It didn't get too many channels, and sometimes it was hard to get a good picture, but we didn't care. The fact that we could see a picture with a voice was better than just sitting around listening to the radio. Daddy would send the boys outside to turn the antenna and holler out the window, "Turn it a little more to the right, hold it right there -- okay, stop." He did this every time the reception was not clear. Daddy let us watch the news and sometimes *Bonanza, The Ed Sullivan Show,* and *The Lawrence Welk Show,* but we were never allowed to touch it without Daddy's okay.

I had spent years watching the black Indian boy, but when spring 1963 came around, I got the nerve to talk to him. His name was Leroy. Years earlier he was kind of short and chubby but cute. At fourteen, he had thinned out a bit and grown a couple of inches taller, but he was still cute. He was well-developed and because he worked outside painting houses, the sun had tanned his skin, a bronze tone that made him even more handsome. His hair was jet black, thick and wavy with a curl hanging down the center of his face. *If only my hair could do that...wishful thinking.* Leroy was handsome -- very handsome, and he knew it, but he wasn't arrogant at all. I guess looks didn't matter to him or he wouldn't have been interested in me. Leroy was a year younger than me but he acted like a grown man. He had quit school and never went back, but he was smart. He was the smartest boy I ever met, and he had a real job like Daddy. Leroy was handsome but he smoked like a freight train. He said he been smoking since he was nine years old and he was good at it. He could blow smoke out of his nose and from his nose to his mouth. He could even blow perfect circles from his mouth and make them spread like little clouds. I asked what his daddy and mama thought about him smoking. He said "It don't matter, I'm a man now. You want to try it?"

"Why not?" I said. He passed the homemade cigarette to me; I inhaled, swallowed the smoke, and like to choke to death.

"You all right?" he asked. When he saw that I was okay, he started demonstrating the correct way to smoke a cigarette.

"I'll pass, that about killed me." I knew that day I would never smoke another cigarette in my life. Leroy gave up on trying to get me to smoke. He said he didn't want his woman smoking no way. When I heard him say "his woman," my mind went back to Mo'n and Daddy telling me I'm a woman. Now, Leroy was calling me his woman. Lord, what did he mean by that? He never asked me if I wanted to be his woman in the first place, but he did ask me if I could receive company. *Receive company, what is that?* He knew I didn't know what he meant, so he asked if he could come see me. My heart skipped two beats. I didn't know how Daddy and Mo'n would feel about that and I wasn't ready to find out, so I told him I couldn't. I could tell he didn't like my answer, but he left that subject alone.

Sunday evening a week later, we all was sitting out on the front porch when Leroy walked up our steps and onto the porch where we were. He acknowledged Mo'n and Daddy and proceeded to ask Daddy if I could receive company; my heart about came through my shirt. It never crossed my mind that he would come and ask Daddy anything. He had some nerve, stepping his feet on our porch like he was my Daddy's friend. Daddy looked at him in amazement and said to me, "Nadine, Mr. Leroy here wants to court you, what you think about that?" My eyes bugged and my heart just stopped beating, I didn't know what to say -- or think, for that matter; I just froze.

"Nadine, I'm talking to you."

"Yes sir."

"Yes sir what?"

Just bury me alive, what in the hell do you want me to say, I don't know nothing about courting. Looking down, I said, "Sir, I don't know what courting is."

Daddy looked at Leroy, "Nadine don't know what courting is, so you need to get your yellow ass back down them there steps the same way you came up them and I don't want to see you around here, you hear me?"

He said, "Yes sir," and walked down the steps the same way he came up.

When he got halfway down the steps, Daddy said, "I don't want to see you around here again until next Sunday. Sundays, you hear me?"

"Yes sir."

Leroy smiled from ear to ear and jumped the last two steps and ran home. I almost fainted.

"Nadine, fetch me a tall glass of ice water."

"Yes sir."

I stumbled into the house in a daze, wondering what had just happened. I admired Leroy for not being afraid to face Daddy. And he did it because he wanted to court me, Nadine Thomas. *Nadine got a boyfriend*. Who would have thought? Not me! When I opened the screen door and went in the house, I overheard Daddy say, "I like that light-skinned nigger. He ain't afraid to look me in the eye."

Leroy and I were allowed to court on Sundays. He came over around three o'clock in the afternoon and we sat in the living room with Daddy or Mo'n right there to make sure Leroy didn't get too grown for his britches. We didn't sit close; he sat at one end of the sofa and I sat at the other. I knew better than to try to sit close to him. Mo'n would have wrung my neck right in front of Leroy and kicked him out, and I didn't want that because I had it hard for Leroy. I think he felt the same for me, but I really didn't know what he saw in me. Leroy always dressed his best when he came over to the house. He said he did it for me, but I think he wanted to impress my Daddy. He would wear a pair of dark britches with a starched crease down the center of each leg, a buttoned dress shirt with a collar, and his Sunday shoes. During the week he wore white painter pants, a white shirt and black work boots his Uncle Clinton gave him when he came back from the war. I never understood how he never got paint on his clothes when he was painting. Leroy said it was the mark of a great painter and I believed him. He had to be a good painter; he learned to paint from his daddy, who learned to paint from his daddy.

We courted all through the summer and winter months and when springtime came around again, we started sneaking and meeting without Daddy or Mo'n's knowledge. In the back of Leroy's house they had all kinds of fruit trees. They had a peach tree, a pear tree, and an apricot tree. I had some nerve being out there alone with Leroy. If Mo'n had known, she would have beat the smut off me, but I didn't care no more because Leroy liked me and I damn sure liked him. I liked being with Leroy; he had an old soul. Old folks would say he had been here before. I can't explain that saying, but I did understand what they meant. I read in a book somewhere, they call it reincarnated.

Of all the trees, the peach tree was our tree; it was a tall and wide tree. Leroy said his granddaddy planted the tree. He said the tree was more than 80 years old. I didn't know anything could bear fruit at that age. But again, I read in the Bible that Sarah had a baby at 90, so it's possible, and the tree did bear some good peaches. The peaches weren't like the picture-perfect peach you see at the local fruit stands. They were small in size, yellow, and had little black specks on them, but they were so good. The more specks they had on them, the better they tasted. When the tree was full of fruit, Leroy and I would sit and rest our backs against the trunk of the tree. We would eat peaches and talk about everything. Leroy had a loving family; I longed for a family like his, but that was not the hand I was dealt. I never talked about my family, because I believe if you ain't got anything good to say about your family, you shouldn't say anything at all. I just kept my mouth closed on that subject. Meeting under that tree became a Friday evening thing and the second time I met him there, he told me to sit down next to him and he started rubbing his hand down my left thigh and I froze. My eyes got big as 50-cent pieces and I didn't know what to do. *Should I strike out running?* He knew I was scared and he assured me he wasn't going to hurt me.

"Am I hurting you Nadine?" I never looked at him; I kept nervously looking straight ahead and shook my head. "Relax, I ain't gonna hurt you, I love you." *Did he just say he loved me? Is this what love feels like? Because rubbing my thigh is feeling good to me.* I was still scared. "Do you want me to stop, Nadine?" *You don't really expect me to respond.* I couldn't say a word because my heart had jumped from my chest to my mouth. He said, "Just close your eyes, Nadine, and relax. I just wanna make you feel good; I want you to feel my love for you." The way he said my name put me in a trance. When I closed my eyes, he pulled my skirt up. *Oh shit!* I wanted to hit his hand but I wanted to feel his love too; besides, I was too scared to open my eyes so I closed them tighter. He pulled the elastic on my panties and put his hand on my privates. *I'm so glad I changed my drawers this morning. I had put on a pair with the elastic coming loose and a hole in them.* I jumped and he said, "Do you trust me, Nadine?" *Did I answer you the last couple of times? What makes you think I'm going to answer you now?* I knew he didn't expect me to answer him. I was about dizzy then; nobody had ever put their hand on my privates except me when I washed. Before I could hear myself think, Leroy had inserted a finger into my privates. *Oh shit, I better get up and run before he gets me pregnant.*

"Leroy, stop before I come up pregnant."

"You can't get pregnant like this," he said in a tone so calm, as he moved his fingers around on the inside of me. It felt so good, I forgot about Mo'n and Daddy for a minute. It felt so good, I wanted to scream. I wanted his love to last forever, but after about a minute, a vision of Mo'n came to me and I remembered how Daddy had put Big Sister out in the street so I jumped up and ran home. He came that next Sunday but I couldn't face him, so at three o'clock I pretended I was sick and Mo'n sent him home. His sticking his finger in me felt so good, I must be pregnant. If Leroy got me pregnant I didn't know what I was going to do. *Lord, please forgive me of my sin and don't let me be pregnant, I won't ever let Leroy put his finger inside me again no matter how good it feels. Please Lord, please.* I felt at peace after confessing to God. God knew my heart, so He knew I was just saying that at the moment, and that I was going to do it again and ask for His forgiveness again. I just hoped I didn't go to meet my Maker before I asked for forgiveness and really meant it.

That following Friday, I didn't meet Leroy under the peach tree. I didn't see him again until two Sundays later. Daddy really liked him and he started letting us sit alone in the living room. But not before he warned Leroy he was in the next room. Leroy was so daring, and as soon as Daddy walked out he touched me and I jumped. *You need to keep your hands to yourself.* He laughed and said "What's wrong?"

I whispered "Look, Leroy -- I like you a lot, but I can't get pregnant. I've been scared out of my mind; we shouldn't be doing grown folk things."

Leroy busted out laughing "Nadine, you think…" he couldn't finish what he wanted to say for laughing so hard. He thought it was funny; I didn't think it was a laughing matter, and I rolled my eyes at him. When he saw I was serious he said, "Nadine, you are so naïve -- you got to do more than what I did to you to get pregnant. You probably think babies come from a log, too, don't you?"

"Well, don't they?"

"Nadine, I see I got to teach you some things cause you my woman." Hearing him say I was his woman made me feel light-headed. I was persuaded that light-skinned Indian boy had feelings for me, and the feelings were mutual.

Chapter Seven

I had been hanging out under the peach tree with Leroy when Daddy called for me. He had called us each by name and when he called me I looked at Leroy and gathered myself. "Lord, what if he seen me under this peach tree?" Scared, I ran across that field, jumped the brook, and ran around the house to the front yard and climbed the steps like never before. I forgot I was scared of the steps, I climbed them so fast.

"What took you so long? When I call you I 'spect you to come ASAP, you hear me?"

"Yes sir."

"Now get in here -- the Reverend Dr. Martin Luther King, Jr. is getting ready to speak on television; he up there in Washington DC."

That was easier than I thought. I'm so glad Daddy didn't send one of the boys to find me. I walked in the house behind Daddy and I felt Mo'n's eyes fixed on me.

"Gal, where you been at? I didn't see you out in that back yard where you said you would be."

Before I could conjure up a lie, Daddy told her to be quiet – Dr. King was about to approach the podium. She rolled her big buckeyes at me and said, "I'll get it out of you later, one way or the other." Blood rushed to my head when Mo'n said she would get it out of me later. I had until Dr. King finished his speech to come up with something. There was no way I was going to tell Mo'n I was under that peach tree with Leroy. After she was finished with me, I would think twice about being under any tree again but I would do it again because when I remembered the love I felt there with Leroy, it was worth any ass whipping Mo'n would ever give me.

When Dr. King walked up to the podium, you could hear a pin drop in that room. Everybody was quiet because they wanted to hear, and we knew not to speak anyway after Daddy's told us to be quiet. But I was quiet because I was trying to think of what lie I was going to tell Mo'n to save my life. Dr. King started out speaking in a monotone voice as if he had selected his words for the speech carefully, but the crowd was responding with so much emotion, he started preaching. His voice began to rise and fall just like the Baptist preacher he was. He reminded me of Pastor Dixon, but he spoke with a little bit more intelligence. Where Daddy was Pastor Dixon's cheerleader, the mass of people in Washington -- a number no man could count -- cheered Dr. King on. Daddy, Mo'n, and we children found ourselves even responding to the television. I didn't forget I had to answer to Mo'n, but I just didn't care at that moment. Dr. King did not even look down at his notes. When he finished his "I Have a Dream" speech, everybody in the room and the all the people on the television were silent. I think we all were overcome by his words. I can remember his speech as if it was yesterday. After a few moments of silence, the crowd on the television began to cheer and weep openly, blacks and whites together. We cried too. There wasn't a dry eye in that living room that day. Even Mo'n, who I didn't think was capable of crying, was crying, which to my knowledge was a first. We sat for a while in silence. To lift

our spirits, Daddy told us we all could go back outside. I knew he
wasn't talking to me, so I remained sitting.

When Mo'n saw me sitting she said, "Go on out, Nadine, but
don't you leave this yard."

I said an outward "Yes, ma'am." *Thank you, Dr. King, for saving
me*. When I opened the screen door and walked out on the porch,
the other children were still on the porch. They had an opportunity
to go wherever they wanted to go, but all we wanted to do was sit
on the porch and reflect on Dr. King's speech. I remember looking up and down the street, and no one else was out playing either.
There was calmness in the air throughout the neighborhood. My
guess was everyone was still glued in front of their television.

The older black folks thought of Dr. King as the "Great Black
Hope." Both young and old started reciting portions of his "I Have
a Dream" speech. Black folks needed a change; hell I knew I needed
one, and I understood how they felt. A year later, a song came out
titled "A Change Is Gonna Come," and it became the anthem for
the Civil Rights Movement. People played that song in their homes,
in the juke joint and even at church when the occasion warranted it.
Mo'n never asked me again what took me so long to get home, and
I kept meeting Leroy on Friday evenings under the peach tree and
receiving him on Sunday afternoons.

In the sixties, folks down South got tired of not being able to
find work, and started moving up North to look for jobs. Esther
moved too, and I was glad she was gone with her mean ass. Even
though I had been doing my own hair for a while by then, she was
still low-down. She was an old maid when she went North and
hadn't been there more than two weeks before she married some
Northerner. She had to be desperate, because from the pictures she
sent Mo'n of her with her husband, he looked like a sissy boy. It was

just like Esther to marry somebody she could manhandle, because no real man was going to put up with her shit. Mo'n talked about her like she was the best thing since white bread. I heard her tell Cousin Jessie Bell that Esther and her husband, Larry, lived in a big house in a good neighborhood and that she worked but her husband took good care of her. Esther had bragged that Larry played the piano for their church and she was one of the soloists in the choir. They even had a piano at their house; Esther sent a picture of herself standing by the piano. She sent other photos as well, posed by other pieces of furniture in her house. She always wanted to be a big shot. Esther rarely came home for a visit, thank God. She told the boys and Sarah that jobs were plentiful up there, and that if they wanted to come when they finished high school they were welcome to come. All the boys except Isaiah went north and never looked back. The only thing holding Isaiah back was graduation. He had plans to go north as soon as he was out of school. Esther never offered me to come, but I wouldn't have gone if she had. I wasn't going to leave the only person that had love for me: Leroy.

With the boys gone North with Esther, that left Isaiah, Sarah, and me in the house. Big Sister was now living in Macon County and attending nursing school. Daddy said Macon County was about twenty miles from Opelika. Twenty miles must be a long distance from here because Big Sister never came for a visit like she told me she would.

We returned home from church one Sunday in 1965 and before we could get out of the car, a neighbor, Ms. Essie Bee, in a panic, hollered over to Daddy and told him to turn his television to the news on Channel Nine. Normally, on the Lord's Day, Daddy didn't turn on the television until after the sun set. But when she said news at one o'clock in the afternoon, he knew it had to be important. Back then the community kept each other informed, especially on civil rights issues, so something had to have happened that black folks needed to know about. Daddy ran up the steps two at a time and we followed. When he turned the television on, they were showing footage of the state troopers and local police attacking a crowd of black folks on a bridge. I'll never forget that day; it was March 7th. "Look at this -- Lord Jesus, how long, Lord, how long?" Daddy sobbed. What could they have done to deserve that terrible treatment? They were using tear gas, clubs, and an electric thing farmers used on their cattle, on the black folks. They didn't even care that children were in the crowd.

It started in Marion, Alabama, somewhere near Selma; a family was protesting for the right to vote, when a woman pushed a white trooper off her 82-year-old father, whom the trooper was beating. When she did that, several white troopers started beating the woman. When her son defended her, they beat and shot him. The son died, and blacks were fed up and took to the street. The crowd was walking from Selma to Montgomery, Alabama to complain to Governor George Wallace, but as soon as they crossed the bridge that led out of Selma, they were told to turn around. Instead of turning around, they knelt to the ground to pray and were attacked. Segregation was alive in the south. It existed in Opelika too, but we didn't experience all the fighting and killings like the other cities in the state. Daddy used to say it was because black folks in Opelika stayed in their place, but I have since come to realize the white folks knew there were some crazy Negroes in Opelika and we were not going to take injustice lying down. What we witnessed that day was a crying shame. No one deserved to be treated that way; no one.

They called it "Bloody Sunday," and it was. Things just couldn't continue as usual. They played that broadcast over and over that day and we watched it over and over and were angered by what we saw. Daddy was fit to be tied. "God is my witness, if I had been there, they may have kilt me but I would have took some of them Crackers down with me. The folks were praying, for God sakes!"

I felt the same way at the moment, but I don't know if I would have had the courage to die for the cause if I had to. The tone of Daddy's voice told me he meant every word he said.

Chapter Eight

I turned seventeen in June and got a weekend job at a little juke joint called Ballerina Inn. The Ballerina Inn was a brown wooden house with a porch low enough to step up on without using the two concrete steps. It had three rooms: a big dance hall, a storage room that also served as an office for Mr. Wright, the owner, and one bathroom that the men and womenfolks used. There was only one way in and out, unless you used the windows. Two windows on one side of the room were propped open with sticks to let a breeze in on hot summer nights, and during the winter when the place was packed like a can of sardines and smelling tired. All the floors were wooden, and although the dance floor was swept nightly, it always looked like it needed to be swept. Situated around the room were about ten mismatched tables and chairs in all colors, shapes, and sizes. An old worn jukebox sat in a corner next to the bar, and for a quarter, you could play ten songs. Everybody that came to the Inn had the blues because all I ever heard coming out of that jukebox was good ole down home blues. The words in those songs expressed what I was feeling. Daddy called it devil music. He would have called the Inn a whorehouse if he knew Mr. Wright used red light bulbs in the dance hall. I worked there on Friday and Saturday nights. They were closed on the Lord's Day but if they weren't, I wouldn't be there because Daddy wouldn't let me work if I wanted to. I enjoyed working there; it gave me a chance to get out of the house on weekends.

I looked forward to Friday night because not only did I get to go to work, Leroy always came and hung out so he could walk me home. He would sit in a corner, and when he wasn't rolling his Prince Albert tobacco, he had his pocket knife out, chipping wood off a limb he got from some tree. He said it was his walking stick but he never used it to help him walk; his legs were fine. Leroy would sit at a table in the corner puffing one cigarette after another like a chain smoker, minding his own business and looking at me. He always watched me while I served drinks, and it made me feel special. I wasn't old enough to serve drinks, but I did. Mr. Wright had already told me what to do if the law came in -- put the liquor down and act like I was there to party with the rest of them. Leroy didn't say a lot to anybody; he only spoke when he was spoken to, although when he was with me he had a whole lot to say and do.

One night at work, a drunk put his arms around my waist. I didn't appreciate him doing that, but I realized he was drunk so I tried to be nice and gently took his arms from around me. As I walked off, he pinched me on my butt and really pissed me off. I turned around and told him to keep his got damn hands to himself. He said, "You ugly bitch, you oughta be glad somebody wants to touch your nappy head ass."

I didn't respond to what he said, because what he said was true; I had heard it for years from my own Mo'n. I hung my head and walked back to the bar trying to pretend the drunk's words didn't bother me, but in reality they hurt. Leroy had been watching the whole time, I guess to see how I was going to handle the situation.

I didn't see Leroy coming, but he ran up to the man and put his pocket knife against his neck.

"I will cut your motherfuckin' neck off, if you ever touch or speak to my woman like that again." I was so scared that night -- the tone of his voice sounded like he meant what he was saying. I had never seen him this way before; he was mad. I didn't want him to kill that man and go to prison, but I was too scared to stop him. Somebody went to the back and got Mr. Wright. Mr. Wright wouldn't approach Leroy either, but from a distance he tried to talk Leroy into letting the man go. That drunk sobered up quick and pissed all over himself as he pleaded with Leroy for his life. Mr. Wright told Leroy he didn't need any trouble around the Inn, because the law was looking for a reason to close his place down. Leroy didn't say a word; he just released the man and walked back to his seat in the corner. Men and womenfolks started whispering, "That bastard is crazy."

"That whole family is crazy."

"Them Indians don't play; his daddy cut a man up a few years ago."

I don't know if there was any truth to what they were saying and still don't today, but I was glad he was on my side that night. That night, I felt, if no one else in the world loved me, Leroy did -- and I felt so much love for him.

That night, Mr. Wright allowed me to lock up the Inn for him. He trusted me a lot and knew it would be okay for him to go on home because Leroy was there to walk me home. He paid me a little extra to sweep and clean the dance hall after it closed. Leroy and I hadn't said a word to each other since before the confrontation with the drunk. When everybody left, I walked back to the storage room to get a broom and when I returned, Leroy was locking the windows. Just as I started sweeping the floor, he walked up to me and without saying a word, took the broom and started to sweep the floor. I went behind the bar and started wiping it down. When I looked across the room at Leroy, there was something so peaceful about him; he didn't look like he would hurt a fly, or like the man who had threatened to cut that drunk's head off a few hours earlier. He swept the floor as if he was in a world of his own.

Watching him mesmerized me and when he felt me staring, he looked over and it was too late for me to turn away. We looked at each other for what seemed like forever. He had charmed me like the cat had charmed that snake in our backyard years earlier. I was locked in on him, and had he not smiled just a little and started back sweeping, we might have been there all night looking at each other. Leroy was beautiful. Everything about him was beautiful. And I was glad he was mine. When we finished cleaning, I locked up the Inn and we walked down the dark dirt road, still in silence. With no streetlights or cars passing to give off light, we walked in total darkness until we reached Ms. Lillie Pearl's house. The light from her porch flickered as if it was about to blow. As we passed her house, Leroy took my hand and we walked hand-in-hand. I figured I should be the one to break the silence.

"Thanks for sticking up for me like that."

"Ain't no bastard gonna disrespect my woman. You don't do no shit like that. He lucky I let him live."

I was already thinking about the things I heard the folks saying back at the club so I asked, "Did your daddy cut a man up?"

"Yeah, but the bastard lived." I was horrified. He sensed his comment scared me, so he laughed and said he was just joking. I didn't think it was a joke, but I was glad to let it go.

I wanted to show him how thankful I was, so I said, "Do you

want to do it?" *Am I crazy? I did not just ask Leroy if he wanted to do it!*

"Yeah, if you want to." I wanted to and I didn't. I was expecting him to say he didn't feel up to it. I don't know why I expected him to say that. I couldn't change my mind now.

"Okay." He led me into the bushes, on the side of the dirt road; my old playground. I once went in the same bushes with my brothers and sister to pick blackberries and plums. The thorns on the blackberry bushes would leave scratch marks all over our legs and arms but we were determined to pick those berries and take them home so Mo'n could make us a blackberry cobbler. She would say, "Y'all gonna get enough of going out in them bushes, it's snakes and things out there." We had seen a few snakes and run like crazy, leaping over tall bushes, in case we crossed another snake's path while we were trying to get away. I guess the saying "God looks out for young folks and fools" is true, because it didn't stop us from going back the next time we wanted blackberries and plums. *I am going back in the bushes with Leroy.* I wanted so bad to ask God to look out for me, but I wouldn't dare. I just hoped He would anyway. We walked a good ways into the bushes and Leroy took his jacket off and laid it down. He told me to lie down on his jacket. I sat down on it and he said again, "Lie down." I wasn't used to lying down; we normally did it sitting up, but I closed my eyes and did what he said, and he got down with me. When he hiked my skirt up and pulled down my panties, I wondered why he didn't just pull them to the side, so I opened my eyes to find Leroy had taken off his britches.

"Leroy, what are you doing?!" He put his hand on my mouth.

"I ain't gonna hurt you. Nadine -- close your eyes."

"Why you take off your britches? You didn't do that before when we did it."

"Just trust me, okay?"

I lay there stiff as a doorknob with my eyes shut tight as he climbed on top of me. I didn't understand why he had to put all his weight on me to put his finger in me and I almost panicked, thinking I wouldn't be able to catch my breath. When he got on top of me I could still breathe, so I didn't freak out. Leroy was lying on top of me and he kept putting his hand down by my privates, but he never inserted his finger. It wasn't long before I realized he wasn't trying to put his finger in me, he was trying to put his thing in. My nature was rising but I still didn't like how it felt and longed for his finger. His thing was too big to go in me because each time he tried, it slid between my thighs. After a while, he let it stay between my thighs and started humping up and down. After a while, I realized Leroy thought he had his thing inside of me and I didn't tell him no different. When he finished I was so wet down there. He let me wipe myself with his jacket. *I hope his mama ain't got to wash this jacket*. We straightened ourselves up and walked back out onto the road.

As we walked to the house he said, "Nadine baby, you sho got a big hole -- I hope I didn't hurt you?" *If you putting your thing in between my thighs was all to doing it, I could handle that*. I told him it didn't hurt. I just didn't like the mess it made and I preferred his finger more. But that night he was happy, so I was too. Doing it became a Friday and Saturday night thing and I soon found out, his thing really did go in my privates. It hurt, too -- and I wasn't going to do it again, but Leroy promised it wouldn't hurt the next time. Not only was he right, but it felt better than his finger. I wanted him in me whenever possible; I loved to feel his love. I didn't know I was capable of experiencing love like that, but I was still concerned about getting pregnant. Leroy promised he wasn't going to get me pregnant and told me to trust him and I did, with all my heart.

Chapter Nine

Something had been going on with my Daddy. He was drinking an awful lot lately. So much so, it was taking a toll on his health. I overheard Mo'n tell him he was going to drink himself to death if he didn't stop. Most of his drinking those days had been with Mr. Henry. Mo'n told Cousin Jessie Bell that as soon as the whistle blew for Daddy to get off, he and Mr. Henry drank. The liquor store was right across the street from Daddy's work site, and they drank liquor like it was water. Every since I was a little girl, I never remembered Daddy drinking in the house. It was as if our house was sacred back then -- now it didn't matter to Daddy anymore. His drinking really bothered Mo'n, and Daddy knew it, but it seemed the more she said something, the worse he got. He would stand in the center of the living room and sing "I drink gin, gin cause it ain't no sin!" He swallowed it without a chaser. He had started leaving the house on Saturday evenings and not even bothering to return until early Sunday morning, just as we were getting ready to eat breakfast. It didn't matter if he had a hangover, he went to church.

One Sunday morning when he got in, he was looking forward to going to church. Pastor Dixon had told him at Wednesday night Bible Study, the deacons had called a special meeting after service the following Sunday. Mo'n begged Daddy to stay home from church because she didn't want to be embarrassed by him. He told her he was going and when Mo'n told him she wasn't going with him, he said, "You might not go, but my churins going." He told us to get up from the breakfast table and go get dressed so we could leave. I know Mo'n wanted to say something, but she knew when it came to Daddy and his children, she wouldn't win. She might have labored to have all nine of us, but we were his property. He said he was the one that would have to give an account to the Lord for how he raised his children, so we went on to church.

At church, during the service, Deacon Jones, a stout man who wore thick Coke-bottle glasses and a buttoned suit jacket so tight that if he took a deep breath all the buttons would pop off, got up from the Deacons' corner located on the left side of the church and walked to the podium, which was over on the right side where the Deacon Wives sat, and gave the church clerk a special announcement. The length of his pants stopped well above his ankles and he wore white thick socks with two red stripes at the top of them, which made his feet look like they were stuffed into his Sunday shoes. Deacon Jones had a dandruff problem too; he had flakes on the shoulders of his jackets every Sunday. He should have taken a lesson or two from Daddy on how to dress for church. But when it came to the Lord, one thing for sure I knew about Deacon Jones, he was serious about the Lord's business. He had told the church clerk to read the announcement after the choir sung their A selection. The spirit was high in the sanctuary until the clerk announced the special meeting following the morning worship service.

"The deacons are asking all members to remain in the sanctuary after the visitors leave for a special meeting."

It had been a while since we had a special meeting. The women in the congregation started whispering, trying to guess what young girl was knocked up or who got caught with whose husband. I started thinking to myself, *Leroy and me is doing it but I am not pregnant. I hope nobody seen us coming out of the bushes.* The choir started singing their B selection, "Maybe God Is Trying to Tell You Something," and the murmuring stopped. The women's curiosity vanished as soon as the song leader belted out her first line, "Can't sleep at night." The congregation shouted in response.

"Amen!"

"Sang, sister!"

"Let the Lord use you!"

By the time she got to "And my soul wonders why," you would have thought we were at a pep rally because everybody was up on their feet. That song was an old favorite, and every time the choir sang it, the congregation outsang the choir. The rest of the service went on as usual and Daddy had a good time. He was up on his feet shouting, "Sing, choir!" It got so good to him, he even did a dance. I wouldn't call it a holy dance; that alcohol had him worked up that morning. I don't know why Mo'n was in such an uproar about Daddy going to church drunk; she knew he could hold his liquor. When Pastor Dixon gave the text, Daddy was worn out and his eyelids were heavy. In between Pastor Dixon's voice rising during his sermon, Daddy would wake up and shout, "Preach! Doc! Yes sir!" and go back to sleep. That went on until Pastor gave the benediction.

When the sermon was over and all the visitors were gone, we all assembled back in the sanctuary; the room was packed. There were more people there for the meeting than at the morning worship service. If the clerk had announced it was just a meeting, most folk would have left thinking they wanted volunteers to bring chicken for the chicken dinner sale. The word "special" indicated something more, and members who hadn't come to the morning service, and even some who had not been to church in years, showed up. They had heard about the special meeting and just knew some juicy information was going to be revealed, passed, or voted on. Folks came out the woodwork for this meeting. We were Missionary Baptists; we voted on everything and the majority won. We voted the preacher in and we voted him out. We even voted if someone wanted to be a member. The pastor would say after his little speech, "All in favor of so and so becoming a member of the Friendship Baptist Church, signify by a show of hands." A sea of hands would go up; then out of formality the pastor would ask if there were any nays, and immediately say, "The yes has it." He never really waited to see if there were any nays, and I wondered what they would have done if everybody raised their hands for no. Would they stop that sinner from giving his or her life to Jesus?

Something about that special meeting had Deacon Jones's name written all over it. He had been in Friendship Baptist since he was born. His father was the Chairman of deacons and his mother, president of the deacon wives' auxiliary and the missionary society. Two of his uncles were trustees, and for years they ran the church and the preacher too. Six months earlier, he had got upset because he wasn't voted in as Chairman of the Deacon Board when Deacon Smith went on to be with the Lord. I remember him coming to Daddy and asking him to speak on his behalf, but Daddy wouldn't. I don't think Deacon Jones cared much for Daddy after that. It would not have surprised me if he had called the meeting and called all the other members who hadn't been there in years, and convinced them to come and vote his way.

Deacon Herbert Rivers carried a folding chair and centered it in front of the communion table that served as a centerpiece. The table had a crushed red velvet table runner trimmed in gold with gold tassels, running longways on the table and decorated with a big Holy Bible and red thick candles on either side. The table was more sacred when it was not in use than on first Sunday when we had the Lord's Supper during the noon worship service. I remember when we practiced for the Easter and Christmas program; we would have to stand in front of the communion table. God forbid if one of the children backed up against the table and touched it. Mrs. Queenie, who was over the youth, had a fit. "Don't touch that table!" When Miss Queenie finished yelling at you, if you couldn't remember the lines of your speech before, you surely weren't going to remember them now.

Deacon Jones rang the Sunday school bell to bring the meeting to order. At the sound of the bell, Deacon Rivers set the chair up front. Deacon Jones then started a song, "Sinner Please Don't Let This Harvest Pass." Why do Baptist folks think they have to have a devotional service before every meeting? We had just got out of service. Why Lord, why? Nevertheless, at the end of the first verse, Deacon River proceeded to knelt down on the chair and prayed:

"Our Father which art in heaven; Holy would be thy name, thy kingdom come; right now a few of your believing children, come bowed down with a humbled heart and bowing heads just to say thank you Jesus. You woke us up early this morning and started us on our way. You gave us food and shelter. We look down, we had legs, and we can walk. You gave us eyes so we could see. You gave us a tongue to talk. We realize, Lord Jesus, that you didn't have to do it but I'm glad you did. I'm so glad that you made a way for me Jesus. You been mighty good. Right now Father, I want you to go to the jailhouse and behind the prison walls. Stop by the nursing home Father because you are a healer, you a bright and morning

star. Can't nobody do you like Jesus. He is a midnight rider. He'll be your doctor in a sick room. He'll be your lawyer in the courtroom. He'll be a friend when you need Him. And somebody need you today, Lord. Lord, I realize that when I laid down my head last night, the bed I slept in was not my cooling board. I thank you, Jesus, that you stayed up on the cross and you didn't say a mumbling word. You stayed right there, all day Friday. You stayed there, all day Saturday. But somebody said on Sunday morning, you got up out the grave with all power in your hand. Lord, when we've sung our last song; and prayed our last prayer, I want you to give us a home somewhere in your kingdom. Where the wicked shall cease from troubling and the weary shall be a rest. Let the church say amen."

"Amen!"

Personally, I wanted to scream, but I didn't want the ushers who had retired from their duties to think I had caught the spirit. After the prayer, Deacon Rivers got up sweating something awful and I really hoped the Lord heard him because he laid it all on the altar. He stood behind the chair like the ushers did when the pastor opened the doors of the church. The doors weren't literally opened, but if you wanted to come to Jesus and join the church, you could, and the ushers were there to direct you to your seat. When he had taken his post, Deacon Jones spoke. "First giving honor to God, Pastor Dixon and all the members of this household of faith." *Excuse me, but my Daddy is still sitting up in the pulpit. He is an associate minister at this church. Deacon Jones, you wrong for that.* "The deacon board has come before you this here afternoon cause one of the brethren has fallen from grace." *A brother?* It was normally a young girl being forced to confess her sins before the church and ask the congregation of hypocrites for forgiveness. With a smirk on his face, Deacon Jones said, "Reverend R. L. Thomas, come down front and face the charges against you." *He did not just ask my Daddy to come down and face charges*!

At first, Daddy just sat there. After a few seconds he realized Deacon Jones had called his name and he stood straight up, straightened his suit, and walked up to the podium. He looked down at Deacon Jones and Deacon Rivers, who was still standing behind the folding chair, and said, "Who, me? I'se Reverend Robert Lewis Thomas, a man of the cloth, and you gonna bring me fore the church? The devil is a liar!"

Pastor Dixon said, "Reverend, hear him out. The Bible tells us if thy brother trespass against thee, rebuke him; and if he repent, forgive him."

"That don't 'ply to me -- I'se a reverend, not just a member!"

"Brother, God is no respecter of persons."

I wanted to crawl under the pew where we were sitting and disappear. Mo'n must have known something was up, and that was the reason she stayed home. I wondered how she would have handled this situation. Daddy could have used her support at that moment in time. Who else could vouch for this man of the cloth? "So you mean to tell me, you gonna 'llow this to continue, Pastor?" Daddy said. Before Pastor Dixon could respond, Daddy grabbed his overcoat and headed for the swinging wooden double doors that led to the vestibule. When he reached the pew where we were sitting he said, "Isaiah, Sarah, and Nadine -- let's go, now, damn it!" I guess we didn't move fast enough because Daddy said damn it right there in the church. Pastor Dixon got up and followed Daddy and us out, trying to reason with him, but Daddy was furious.

"Reverend, you been here at Friendship Baptist a long time, I'm sure it's some kind of misunderstanding and you will be able to set the record straight yourself, if you stayed."

"I ain't staying to set shit straight!"

Lord, please don't strike my Daddy down. As we exited into the vestibule, Deacon Jones shouted something about Daddy having no business sitting up in the pulpit with the lifestyle he had been living for years, because the pulpit was holy. All I heard was loud murmuring from those in attendance. They were ready to hear the charge against Daddy. "R. L., you can run but you can't hide. God knows and sees everything, you hear me! He sees everything, R.L.!" Deacon Jones shouted.

Pastor Dixon tried his best to get Daddy to come back in the church that Sunday. Daddy opened the car door and got in; we followed. Pastor told him the house of God is where sinners come to get things right and that he shouldn't leave God's house mad. He said no man knows the day or the hour when his life will be required of him. He pleaded with him not to leave the church mad and said what if the next time he entered the church doors, the undertaker was bringing him in? Daddy looked at him as if he wanted to cuss him out, but he held his peace and drove off. I wanted him to stay and set the record straight. Daddy was so mad, although he didn't even know the charge against him -- or did he? What did Deacon Jones mean when he said, "You can run but you can't hide cause God see and knows all?" In the midst of all that was going on, my mind stayed on God and the fact that He really does see and know all; He even knew what I had been doing with Leroy. I quickly dismissed that thought, because this was about my Daddy. Was Deacon Jones talking about Daddy's drinking? Hell, everyone knew that Baptist preachers and deacons drink and smoke. Deacon Jones is one to talk, when he lights his cigar on the church ground. Ain't that a sin too?

We drove all the way home in silence. Daddy was drunk when we left the house earlier that morning but he had sobered up since the altercation back at the church. When we turned the corner, Mo'n was sitting on the front porch. She looked like she knew something had happened. Daddy drove up in front of the house but didn't get out of the car, so we didn't either. We weren't moving until Daddy said move. After a minute he told us to go on in the house. We got out of the car and climbed the steps to the porch. Mo'n said, "Go on in there and take off your Sunday clothes."

We were teenagers and we still had to change our clothes after church. She waited for Daddy to come up on the porch and when he did, she asked how service was. He acted as if he didn't hear her, opened the screen door, and walked into the house. Mo'n got up and followed him. "Do you want me to fix you somethin to eat?" He took off his suit jacket, threw his keys on the coffee table, and headed back toward the door without saying a word.

"R. L., where you gwine?"

"I'm-a walk down to Magdalene."

"For what, R.L.? This is the Lord's day!"

The tone Mo'n used, shocked Daddy. She had never used that tone with Daddy. This had to be Mo'n and Daddy's first fight that I can remember. He stopped, looked at her for a few seconds, and walked out the door, but Mo'n wasn't backing down. I remember the day Daddy put Big Sister out. Mo'n didn't feel this strong when he put her out on the street. She followed him out. "So now you gonna drink on the Lord's Day too? Can't you at least respect the Lord's Day, R. L.?" He kept walking. When Daddy left walking I went to my room. I didn't want to give Mo'n a reason to beat me.

We didn't wait for Daddy to return home for us to eat dinner that evening. Leroy came over as usual and Daddy still hadn't come home when Leroy left. It was much later when Daddy came home sick and drunk. I don't know how he climbed those steps in his condition, but he did. He stumbled in their bedroom and fell across the bed. Mo'n didn't say a word to him; she got up and got something out of the bathroom medicine cabinet and went in the room and nursed him like the good wife she was to him. Daddy didn't even have dinner; he slept until it was time for him to get up for work Monday morning. That whole week, we acted as if that Sunday never happened. It was obvious Daddy was embarrassed; the week went by quietly.

On Friday morning, Daddy told Mo'n not to cook because he was taking us all out for footlong hotdogs and an ice cream cone. When he got home that evening, he took a bath and instead of going to the bootleggers' houses, he took us all to Story's Dairy Bar for dinner. He didn't leave us like he normally did on the weekend. That was the first time we ever ate out and Mo'n first time not cooking. We were in heaven. We enjoyed being out with Daddy. He was light-hearted and it seemed like Mo'n enjoyed the outing too. When we got back to the house, Daddy gave each of us five whole dollars. He told Isaiah he would take him to get the shoes he needed for baseball when he got off the next day. That evening was surreal. We watched television together that night. I can't remember what show we watched, because we didn't have to be quiet. It felt like that was what family was supposed to do: spend time with each other and laugh together every once in a while. Maybe Deacon Jones calling a special meeting was what we needed for Daddy to get back on track. I went to bed that night full of hope and looked forward to Daddy coming home from work the next day so I could go with him and Isaiah to spend my five dollars.

The next morning, Mo'n got up and fixed a big breakfast. We all ate together before Daddy left for work. She fried some green tomatoes, fatback meat, smoked sausage, biscuits, and my favorite; brims the size of my hand that Isaiah caught fishing in Buck's pond. I love fish and especially brims. I loved drowning a piece in Louisiana Hot Sauce and having to pick a hundred fine bones. Sometimes I would swallow a bone and would have to pack my mouth with biscuits until it went down my throat. That morning at the breakfast table seemed so special. *Lord, let this day be the beginning of us being one big happy family.*

Daddy worked half a day on Saturdays. That afternoon, Mr. Henry showed up at the house, but Daddy had not got home yet. Mr. Henry knew Daddy didn't appreciate any man coming to his house when he wasn't there, so I wondered what he wanted. Mo'n met him at the door and told him Daddy wasn't home. He told her he knew it and that Mr. Turner had sent him. Mr. Henry told Mo'n that Daddy had fallen sick; his lungs collapsed, and he had to be rushed to the county hospital one hour before he was scheduled to get off.

"Lord-a-mercy -- is he gonna be all right, Henry?"

"Viola, I ain't no doctor, but to tell you the truth, it don't look good."

"Henry, would you take me to him."

Mo'n had prepared dinner earlier and we had been waiting for Daddy to come so we all could eat together before we went to get Isaiah his baseball shoes.

"I'm-a go check on your Daddy and bring him home. Nadine, wash your hands, go in them pots, and fix y'all a plate. If I ain't back fore dark, y'all better be in this house with these doors closed. You hear me?"

"Yes, ma'am."

"Don't have nobody in and out my door -- I'm holding you 'sponsible, Nadine."

"Yes, ma'am."

This was the first time Mo'n left the house for us to tend to. Mo'n left with Mr. Henry and after we ate, Isaiah went to his girl-friend Charlestine's house; Sarah said she was going to sit with Ms. Lillie Pearl, but she had become a sneaky something lately, so I don't know if she was telling the truth about going to Ms. Lillie Pearl's house or not. Isaiah said she was going to see the new boy that moved next door. I really didn't care where they were going. I was glad to be left in charge even though Isaiah didn't see it as me being in charge. Before they left the house, I reminded them of what Mo'n said and told them they better not let night catch them outside.

"Nadine, I ain't hard of hearing, I heard Mo'n."

"I'm just reminding you again because I ain't getting no ass whipping because you don't know how to bring your ass from around Charlestine."

The word exchange between me and Isaiah meant nothing to Sarah. She just walked out the house and Isaiah followed. I called Mr. Wright and told him Daddy was in the hospital and I would not be going in to work. He said he pray Daddy would be all right and told me he would see me the following Friday. I was alone in the house and felt a sense of freedom. I would have stayed in the house, but Leroy was on my mind, so I went out the back door and crossed the brook to his house. He was sitting on the porch with his mama. Ms. Ruth was black but nice as ever. That was the first time I had been up close to her. Her skin was the same color as the lady on the grit box; black as mine, but looked smooth as a baby's butt. I hadn't never seen a baby's butt but that's what they say when something is flawless. I didn't realize her hair was so long since she kept it in one plait and twisted in a bun. On this day, the plait was hanging and it reached to her butt when she stood up. I didn't know black-skinned people could grow hair that long. I used a lot of grease on my hair and it was still short and nappy.

At Leroy's house, only four steps led to their porch, not like the fifteen at home. When I walked up and spoke, Ms. Ruth and Leroy greeted me and I took a seat on the second step. I told them about Daddy being taken to the hospital and Ms. Ruth said she would be praying for him. I thanked her for her prayers. I enjoyed talking to her because she was nothing like Mo'n. Why couldn't I talk to Mo'n like that? I found myself wishing Ms. Ruth was my mama, like I had wished for Ms. Lillie Pearl, but that thought changed quick when I realized Ms. Ruth being my mama meant Leroy would be my brother and he wouldn't be able to show me love the way he did, because kinfolks don't do that. So I decided I would be content with things the way they were. After all, Leroy said I was going to be his wife one day, which meant Ms. Ruth would then be family. I sat with Ms. Ruth and Leroy, enjoying their company for four hours. Night began to fall and I knew I better not let it catch me outside Mo'n's door, so I said my goodbyes and started back to the house.

"Hold up, I'm-a care you home," Leroy said. We walked in silence and Leroy took hold of my hand. I looked back to make sure Ms. Ruth wasn't looking because if she was, I was going to snatch my hand back; I didn't want to be disrespectful. She wasn't looking, so I let him hold my hand. Leroy was quiet, which meant he was up to something. When we reached the steps to the back door, I said goodbye.

"I dare you to let me in."

"Boy, I'm not crazy!"

"Come on, Nadine -- be adventurous, nobody will know."

"Isaiah and Sarah will."

"They not even home yet. Go in and see and if they ain't, I can slip in without them knowing. You told me you got your own room now."

"Leroy, you are going to be the cause of my death. Don't you know Mo'n will kill me if she catches you here?"

"She won't; I will be gone before she gets home."

I looked at him and couldn't resist him for nothing in the world. I opened the back screen door and called out for Isaiah and Sarah. They didn't answer and Leroy was ready to rush on in. I stopped him and told him I needed to go in and make sure. I checked and they hadn't come home, so I let him in. We went up to my bedroom and closed the door. Leroy laid me on the bed and climbed on top of me. We still had our clothes on and he was grinding on me; something else new, but I liked it. The grinding stirred up my nature and I wanted him inside me, but he was in no hurry. His thing against me was getting harder. I normally didn't speak doing our love process but before I knew it, I was begging him to put his thing inside of me. He ignored me and kept saying, "You like it -- you like it, don't you?"

Breathless, I said, "Yeah, hell yeah!" While he was grinding on me, he started rubbing on my titties. *You know I don't allow you to touch my titties, oh don't stop.* I just closed my eyes and took all his love in. I forgot I was in Mo'n and Daddy's house, and it didn't matter at that moment in time. While my eyes were closed, Leroy started sucking my right tittie and just stopped. I opened my eyes. "Leroy, what you doing?" He never answered me. I couldn't believe he stopped like that. He got up, took off his britches and drawers, took my panties off, and got back on top of me. I'm glad he did that because I was about to wet my panties. This was different from when we were under the peach tree or out in the bushes. The bed was soft and I was in la la land when I heard the front door opened and closed. *Lord, Mo'n is home and I'm on my way to heaven for real.* All the good feeling I had felt seconds earlier was gone. Leroy was trying to explode inside me but I told him he had to get up.

"I'll be done in a minute."

"Leroy, we don't have a minute, Mo'n and Daddy will be up here in a few seconds."

I tried to push him up but he was too heavy and wouldn't budge. I asked him again and he acted like he didn't hear me, so I pushed him so hard, he fell off the bed and onto the floor.

"Nadine, what you do that for?"

"Shhh, you going to get me killed."

If I thought Mo'n was trying to kill me before, wait until she got hold of my ass this time. Having Leroy in her house and in my bed was a sure death sentence, and I hadn't planned to die like that. When Sarah heard the sound of Leroy hitting the floor, she yelled from the front of the house, "Nadine, gal, you all right?"

Relieved, I yelled back, "Yeah Sarah, I just fell off the bed."

I looked down at Leroy's naked behind still on the floor holding his thing, and started laughing. He didn't think it was funny. I got my panties from behind the bed and fixed my clothes. I told Leroy not to come out until I came to get him. He was fit to be tied because he didn't finish, but I got mine. I smiled for a quick second and then tried to think of how I was going to get Leroy down the stairs and out the back door. I wished we had used the bed in Daddy's study; it had been a long time since he used it and it would have been easier to let Leroy out. When I got to the top of the stairs, I heard sounds from the television. *Thank you Sarah! I got a plan now.* Sarah knew we weren't allowed to touch the television without permission. Sarah was a year older than me but I had always been able to boss her around; that's why Mo'n left me in charge. I really didn't give a damn about her turning on the television, I was more concerned about how I was going to get Leroy out the house before Mo'n, Daddy, or Isaiah came home -- but Sarah didn't know that.

"I'm going to tell Daddy you turned on the television."

"Come on Nadine, I just want to watch what I want to watch for a change."

She got up and started walking toward the television to turn it off and I stopped her. "No need to turn it off now, you might as well enjoy it because you getting an ass whipping when Mo'n and Daddy come home." God knows, I wasn't going to tell Mo'n nothing, so she could beat my ass for Sarah turning the television on.

"It's your week to clean the bathroom; I'll clean it for you tomorrow."

"Tomorrow? What about Monday, Tuesday, and Wednesday?"

"Okay, I'll do it the whole week."

"That ain't enough."

"What, then?"

"Go down to Charlestine's house and tell Isaiah he better get his ass home before Mo'n and Daddy gets here."

"What if Mo'n comes home while I'm gone?"

"Then you get your ass whipped anyway. But if she ain't here when you get back, your ass is saved, so what are you going to do?"

I thought she might not take the bait, so I encouraged her. "If you leave now, Sarah, you can beat them home." Sarah ran out that door and down those steps so fast -- I didn't know her plump tail could move so fast. I followed her out to make sure she didn't turn around and when she was out of sight, I ran back to my room and told Leroy it was clear for him to leave. He was still sitting on the floor naked. He acted like he thought we were going to go at it again.

Looking up at me, he said, "You don't want to finish where we left off, Nadine?"

"Are you a fool? You better get out of here while you can walk out on your own."

He was holding his thing. "Come on Nadine." He was dead serious.

"Hell naw, Leroy -- you got to go!" *Get your naked ass up and get out of Mo'n's house.* When he saw I was not going to give in, he got up and start putting his clothes back on. He was so frustrated he was putting his britches on without his drawers; they were at the foot of the bed. I picked them up and tossed them to him. When I finally got him out the door, it hit me that I really had Leroy up in Mo'n's house; I got weak in the knees. I should have learned my lesson after that close call but that wouldn't be the last time he was up in Mo'n's house. We just used Daddy's study instead of going up to my room.

When Isaiah and Sarah got back to the house, I was sitting in the living room like I had been holding everything down, since I was the one in charge. We watched television and took turns watching out the window for Mo'n and Daddy so we could jump up and turn the television off. The three of us were glued to the television and had forgotten to watch out for Mo'n and Daddy until we heard a car door slam. Isaiah jumped up and cut off the television and we sat on the sofa like zombies. I hoped they hadn't seen the light from the television through the window. What was taking them so long to reach the door? Mo'n must have had to help Daddy up the steps, because it took what seemed like forever for them to climb the steps. Mo'n walked in the house, and she looked different. We were expecting to see Daddy right behind her, but he never came in. I got an eerie feeling something serious was wrong.

"Mo'n Daddy gonna be all right?" Isaiah asked. "Mo'n, can we go and see him tomorrow?"

When he asked that, Mon let out a sound that came up from the pit of her stomach. "R.L. is gone, R.L. is gone!"

We all started crying and hollering. Mo'n sat on the sofa with her pocketbook in her lap, rocking back and forth. We all gathered around her and she put her arms around us; something she had never done to me, and told us everything was going to be all right. We stayed there in the living room together all night; Sarah and Mo'n were on the sofa and Isaiah and I were stretched out on the floor right next to the sofa. When morning came, I woke up to the sound of Mo'n talking to God. I lay there still so I wouldn't interrupt her prayer. She was telling God she couldn't honor Daddy's last request. She was crying so hard, I actually felt sorry for her. What could Daddy have asked Mo'n to do on his deathbed that she couldn't bring herself to do? When she lifted her head, she saw that I was awake. I hope she didn't think I was eavesdropping; I was waking up.

"Mo'n, I can fix us some breakfast."

"No baby, I got it."

God, she called me baby. Does she know it's me, Nadine, she's talking to? My heart skipped a beat and I was beginning to seriously wonder if Mo'n would be all right.

Over the next couple of days everyone came home for the funeral except Big Sister. Surely, she would come to her own daddy's funeral. Daddy died on Saturday and his funeral wasn't scheduled until the following Saturday; a whole week. Why do black folks take so long to bury their dead? It was a week and a half before they buried our neighbor, Mr. Judge. When Daddy's boss man's daddy died, he died on Tuesday and the funeral was the next day, Wednesday. They say white folks had to bury their dead in a hurry because if they didn't they would turn black. I wondered if there was any truth to that.

Daddy's funeral was at eleven o'clock in the morning. It was pouring down rain outside and very cold. It was cloudy that day and the rain showed no sign of letting up. When we drove up to the church, in the funeral home limousine, standing at the top of the steps that led to the church entrance, holding a black umbrella, wearing a red dress, a big red wide-brimmed hat trimmed in black, and a pair of black four-inch heels was Big Sister, waiting on us. I was glad to see her wearing a whore dress. Daddy never allowed us to wear red; he said whores wear, red but Big Sister didn't look like a whore to me. Standing beside her were two boys: one, David, looked to be about seven years old, and A.J. four. I wondered why her husband, Albert, didn't come. She might have been too embarrassed to bring him; he was twenty years older than she was and I heard Mo'n say he looked every bit of it. She's someone to talk; Daddy was much older than her. I guess Big Sister took marrying an older man after Mo'n.

When we got out of the car, the funeral director gave us umbrellas. Esther was holding on to Mo'n and they shared one. Her husband walked directly behind them with half of his head covered from the rain and the other exposed. They were at the front of the line as we lined up to enter the church. Mo'n had been in a daze for days. She looked as if she had been sedated. When Big Sister walked down the steps to join us, Mo'n smiled, let go of Esther's hand, and grabbed Sister's hand. I could tell Mo'n letting go of Esther's hand for Sister's didn't sit well with Esther, but she wasn't about to cause a scene that day, so she dropped back behind them and walked with her husband. As we walked in the church, the choir sang, "When We All Get to Heaven." As we walked past Daddy's open casket to view his body one last time, Mo'n almost collapsed, but Big Sister caught her and helped her to her seat. Big Sister was there for her and Mo'n held on.

After the church clerk finished reading the obituary, she took her seat on the Deacon Wives side of the church and Esther walked over to the musician, whispered something to him, and then walked up to the podium. "I've always wanted to sing for my daddy in this church. Daddy, this is for you." She looked over at the musician for him to begin playing and he hit a few keys trying to find Esther's key. When she got frustrated with him, she looked over at her husband, Larry, and he got up from his seat and walked over where the musician was sitting at the piano and the pianist got up from the bench and took a seat next to the church clerk. When Larry was situated, Esther cleared her throat. That must have been his clue to start playing because he played several fancy chords as an intro and Esther opened her mouth and begins to sing "Precious Lord, Take My Hand." She sounded just like Mahalia Jackson and she tore the church up. Folks were shouting so; you wouldn't think we were at a funeral. I held my peace out of respect for my daddy. *Look at her, she is really enjoying this. She thinks she's headlining a concert. Daddy was right about her wanting to put on a show. To bad he's not here to see her. He would drag her ass right back to her seat.*

The service went well; the part that I remember. I sat there and my mind kept going back to the last time me, my daddy, Isaiah, and Sarah were at the church and the words Pastor Dixon spoke to

Daddy. Now, not two weeks later, my daddy had to be carried into the church by the undertaker. *I would never know, now, why Daddy was so mad at Deacon Jones, because he took it to the grave with him.* When Pastor Dixon finished the eulogy, the choir sung, "Soon and Very Soon, We Are Going to See the King," as the pallbearers carried Daddy's casket out to the church cemetery. The rain had let up a little and the sun peeped out over the clouds. It was said that the devil was beating his wife when it's raining and the sun is out at the same time. They say if you put a stick to the ground and put your ear to it, you can hear them fighting. I had tried that before and didn't hear anything. Leroy said I used the wrong kind of stick. I looked at that six-foot hole they had dug for my daddy and wondered if I would be able to hear the devil beating his wife if I went six feet down, but I was not going to find out. After the pastor said the last prayer, we walked back to the limousine. As we walked, Mo'n stopped in her tracks and stood there like a cement wall. "I can't leave R.L.; I can't leave him in that cold grave by himself." The boys and Esther pleaded with her, but it was Big Sister who was able to get Mo'n back to the car. *If it was left up to me, Mama dearest, I would help you get in there with Daddy to keep him warm.*

When the limousine dropped us back off at the house, everybody was there. This was the first time we ever had so many people at our house. Daddy didn't allow company except for a few of our friends, Cousin Jessie Bell and those greedy ass preachers. He said folk wanted to be in your business, and he didn't like that. Cousin Jessie Bell didn't like funerals. She said she liked to remember folks as they were when they were alive. She stayed at the house and received the food people from the neighborhood brought over. Ms. Lillie Pearl brought collard greens with ham hocks and a potato pie; Ms. Magdalene, fried some chicken, black-eyed peas and a blackberry pie; Ms. Vernell, a ham and pound cake -- and other folks I didn't know brought chicken, dinner rolls, and sodas. Some folks didn't bring anything; they just stopped by to eat. Cousin Jessie Bell acted as hostess while Mo'n sat with little emotion. I thought she was going to have to be admitted to the crazy house but two days later, she started back talking. Big Sister being there seemed to make it better. She stayed on for a few more days before returning to Macon County; she had to get back to work. She asked Mo'n if her seven-year-old, David could stay and she said yes. She then asked me if I would watch out for him. She didn't have to ask, after all she did for me when she was home. She said her goodbyes to everyone and she and her younger son, A.J., left in her black deuce and a quarter.

By that Friday, my brothers and Esther and her husband left, going back North. The boys took all of Daddy's suits with them. Samuel wanted the car since Mo'n didn't drive, but she told him my Daddy wanted Isaiah to have it. That was good news to Isaiah. Mo'n told them when the insurance money paid off she would send them all a little something.

Chapter Ten

Mo'n stopped being so hard on me after my Daddy died for a while, but she still cussed me out from time to time. I guess she was giving me time to grieve, too. She knew I loved my Daddy. The atmosphere in the house was even lighter. Mon started opening the curtains during the day to let the sun in. She also let us watch television. She kept her promise about buying us a color television when she got the insurance money. She told us still in the home that she had used our share of the insurance money for the color television, and she sent the others a little money. I wanted money too, but I loved the color television. It looked better than the black and white one. We no longer had to use colored cellophane paper over the television to make believe we were looking at a color television. We could see the real colors of the clothes the folks wore. I felt like we had arrived: a color television!

In May, Isaiah and I graduated from high school. Isaiah had packed his suitcase two weeks earlier. He planned to head north the day after graduation. Solomon had told him if he would wait until June, he would come down and help Isaiah drive his car back to Detroit. Isaiah couldn't wait one month; he was ready to leave Opelika. Esther sent him enough money for a Greyhound bus ticket and food to take with him on the bus, and Mo'n gave him a little something too. He told Mo'n he would be back in June to get his car, and he boarded the bus and left.

After Daddy's passing, Mo'n started going up to the Inn with Cousin Jessie Bell on the weekend. She never went out when my Daddy was living; why start now? Her going out meant I could no longer work at the Inn. She said somebody had to be home to care for David. I didn't mind caring for David at all, but I was upset about having to quit because it interrupted Leroy and me stopping in the plum bushes on the way home. But my days were numbered at the Inn anyway because Mr. Wright was concerned that Leroy would kill some man if he looked at me too hard. I think Leroy was starting to be a little jealous; he had said to me before that he would give me what I made at the Inn on his paydays if I quit working there. It wasn't about the money. I loved getting out of the house. Mr. Wright said Leroy had it hard for me, and he had threatened to ban him from the Inn. I was glad Leroy felt that way because I felt the same way about him.

The Inn became Mo'n and Cousin Jessie Bell's stomping ground. It was their regular hang-out place on Friday and Saturday nights, and Mo'n never came home before midnight, so it was safe for Leroy to come over to the house. That ended up working out better than the plum bushes and the hard ground. David and I had a good relationship, and we played a game called "secrets." I told him that whatever happened when Mo'n was gone was between him and me, and Mo'n was never to know. When Leroy came over, he played with David. He was really good with him, so I knew from how he interacted with David that he would be a good father. I never saw Daddy interact with my brothers and playing with us girls was out of the question. When Leroy was done playing with David and we were ready to go to my room, I gave David sweetbread and grape

Kool-Aid -- his favorite -- and let him eat it in the living room while he watched television. Eating in the living room was not allowed, but why not? We had plastic on both chairs and if we spilled something, all we had to do was wipe it off. I told David that Leroy and I were going to the study so we could talk in private and that if he heard someone coming to the front door, he should run to the back and knock on the door three times, but that he was not to open the door. We didn't have locks on the doors at our house -- my Daddy said, it was his house and he should not have to knock on no door in his house to get in. So Leroy and I spent our Fridays and Saturdays together. We had a couple of close calls but we never got caught, thank God, and I still received him on Sundays.

Since Daddy died, Mo'n stopped wearing rags on her head all the time. I wondered if Daddy had her wearing them in the first place. She didn't have a bad grade of hair, and it looked right nice when she fixed it. Some of the menfolks at the Inn must have been trying to get with her, because she even started dressing better. I wondered if that old drunk that put his arms around my waist had tried that shit with Mo'n and if he did, did she like it?

I heard Mo'n tell Cousin Jessie Bell one day, that one Saturday night, when she got home and turned the lights off for bed, the bed started shaking. She said the booger man was trying to get her, but when she got up and turned the light on, it would stop. Mo'n told her she slept with the light on for a month after that. Cousin Jessie Bell told Mo'n that Daddy was getting on her for going out and having too much fun. When Cousin Jessie Bell said that, they laughed so hard Mo'n was crying. *Laugh, Mo'n, laugh, if it keeps you from messing with me; knock on wood.* I must have jinxed myself when I knocked on wood, because her not messing with me didn't last long after that. Out of the blue she asked, "Nadine, did you have your period this month?"

"Yes ma'am."

"Funny thing -- I missed it. I want to see it next month, cause you mess around and get knocked up if you want to, but it's gonna be hell to pay and I'm gonna beat it out of you."

I hadn't had a period in three months but I didn't know that meant I could be pregnant. I thought my body was taking a break. I weighed one hundred and five pounds and didn't look like I had gained weight, although Mo'n had said weeks earlier that I was getting lazy around the house and eating up all her damn food. She got a Social Security check for us the third of each month because of my Daddy; it was our damn food; she didn't work. But she did get a letter from the Social Security office stating that my check would stop now that I was done with school. The thought of being pregnant scared me, and the first chance I got, I ran around to Leroy's house.

"Leroy, I haven't had a period in three months -- what if I am pregnant?"

"Nadine, that don't mean nothing."

"How you know? You do explode inside me, Leroy. What if..."

"Hush, you ain't knocked up. But if you were, you old enough, I will marry you. I told you I love you -- nappy head and all -- and if you having my child, I'm gonna marry you; I can take care of you. I work and get paid every Friday, you hear me?"

I just nodded because I had a feeling he was going to have to put his money where his mouth was. That's an old saying.

The next month came and there was no sign of the red baron. That morning I was sleeping on my side and woke up when I felt something moving inside me. I don't know what made me the most scared; Mo'n finding out I was pregnant, or the fact that something moved inside of me. Big Sister had left a girdle when she was here and I had kept it for years. I didn't know why I had kept it, but I did. I put that girdle on just in case I was pregnant -- I did not want Mo'n to know. I hoped Leroy meant what he said about marrying me, or I'd be up the creek without a paddle. But what I knew for sure was Mo'n wasn't gonna beat a damn thing out of me, because the baby I was carrying came from Leroy's love, and I was going to love and treat it better than Mo'n ever treated me. To protect what is growing in me, I would follow my Daddy to his grave.

As soon as Leroy got off from work, I told him and he was happy. Mo'n being mad never crossed his mind; he wasn't worried about her, but I was. I told him I was scared and he told me not to be. He took my hand and we walked over to the house.

"Leroy, what you fixin' to do?"

"You fixin' to see."

I didn't know what exactly he was going to say to Mo'n, but my blood pressure went up thinking about it. With Leroy holding my hand, we climbed those steps to the front porch, opened the door, and went in. Leroy said, "Good evening, Ms. Viola." Mo'n didn't reply, I think she was surprised to see us holding hands in front of her, because she was looking at our hands. I tried to wiggle my hand loose; Leroy knew it so he gripped it tighter until I gave in.

"Ms. Viola, I'm here to ask for Nadine's hand in marriage." Mo'n was surprised. She asked where we were going to stay if we got married. She said we could not stay with her. It wasn't because she didn't have enough room; the house was big enough. Leroy told her he had talked to his daddy and mama and that we would be staying with his folks until he had us a house built on the land his daddy gave him.

"Oh, is that so?"

"Yes, ma'am."

Mo'n asked me if I wanted to marry Leroy, and I said, "Yes ma'am, I love him. I've loved him for a long time."

"A long time, huh? You don't know nothing about love. Have y'all been fooling around like grown folk?" I froze; I couldn't believe she even asked me that. "Have y'all been doing things grown folk do?" I didn't answer and she yelled, "Nadine, I'm talking to you and if I have to ask you one more time, I'm going knock the hell out of you." I wanted to say something but my mouth wouldn't open.

Leroy squeezed my hand tighter and said, "No disrespect Ms. Viola, but Nadine is eighteen now and we love each other …"

Before Leroy could finish Mo'n interrupted him. "You damn right, no disrespect -- and I ain't talking to you, I'm talking to my child." She looked at me the way she looked when she was getting ready to beat me, and for a split second I felt like the hopeless child she beat unmercifully. "Nadine, I'm gonna ask you one more time." This time when she said it, something rose up in me.

"Yeah Mo'n, we do things grown folks do, and I love the love Leroy gives me. Ever since I was a little girl, I longed for someone to just put their arms around me and tell me they loved me; someone to tell me just once, Mo'n, that I was loved -- and you didn't. I went seventeen years feeling alone. Mo'n, Leroy holds me; he gives me all his love and it explodes inside of me. I tell him I love him and he tells me he loves me too. Mo'n, Leroy loves my ugly, black, nappy head ass and I love him. Now you can give us your blessings if you want to, and if you don't that's fine too. Because I want to be with Leroy and I'm going to marry him with or without your blessings."

I said everything I had been feeling and expected her at any minute to jump on me and beat me into the floor but it would not have mattered because Leroy was holding my hand. When I looked in Mo'n's eyes, she was crying.

"When do y'all want to do this?"

"Tomorrow, ma'am." *Tomorrow! I didn't realize you wanted to do it that quick -- I ain't showing yet* "I work tomorrow but the courthouse is open on Saturday. I want Nadine to meet me there at noon." I looked at him. "That is, if it's okay with you and Nadine."

I stuttered, "I reckon, yes, it is fine with me."

"Well, it's settled," Mo'n said.

"Thank you, Ms. Viola. I better go. Got a big day tomorrow. Nadine, will you walk me out?"

As we walked to the door Mo'n spoke. "Leroy." We stopped and turned to face Mo'n.

"Ma'am?"

"Take care of her."

"I will, ma'am."

Leroy and I walked out on the porch.

"I didn't know you wanted to do it tomorrow, Leroy!"

"What -- you don't want to marry me?"

"Yes, I want to. I just didn't think…"

He stopped me. "Didn't I tell you I would take care of you, Nadine? I meant it. That goes for you and my baby," he said, rubbing the bump I held in when I was around Mo'n. "Now, I want you to put on one of your pretty dresses and meet me at the courthouse tomorrow, okay?" For the first time, we kissed on Mo'n's front porch and didn't care who saw us.

The next morning, I got up early, excited that at noon I would be Mrs. Leroy Washington. Mo'n cooked a good breakfast that morning and offered to straighten my hair. I didn't know whether to be excited or scared, because Mo'n never bothered with my hair. I looked at

Mo'n and remembered the last time Esther straightened my hair with the hot comb. I had to sit, between her legs, on the floor, next to our gas stove so she could reach the hot comb, for close to an hour while she straightened my hair. She burned my ear and scalp more than a few times that morning, and when I flinched she told me to be still -- it was only heat, like I didn't know the difference between heat and being burnt. I remember like it was yesterday the sizzling sound of the Royal Crown grease she packed on my head and how it felt when she burnt me. That was the last time my hair was straightened; I had been wearing an Afro since. Now Mo'n for the first time in my life wanted to straighten my hair. *What's wrong with my Afro? Leroy likes it. What if you burn my scalp? You don't like me no way. This is your way of giving me one last blow before I move out of your house?*

The courage that had risen up in me the night before was gone, and as bad as I wanted to say to her, thanks but no thanks, I didn't. I just prayed that when she finished with my hair, my head would still be there, and it was. For the first time in my life my hair was straight-straight. Even when the others did my hair it didn't come out this good. Straightened, my hair came down to my shoulders. I was so thankful, and I told Mo'n so. Mo'n caught me by surprise when she offered me cab fare to the courthouse and back. I told her Leroy had given me cab fare already. She didn't offer to go with me; I guess she knew I didn't want her to share in the happiest day of my life after all she put me through.

I met Leroy at the courthouse and we went in to the Probate Office and I became Mrs. Leroy Washington; it happened so fast. Leroy was now my husband. Now we wouldn't have to sneak and do nothing, because he was my husband.

Leroy had to get back to work before his lunch hour was over, so he told me to go back to Mo'n's house and pack my things, and he would come over to help me move them when he got off. That wouldn't be necessary because what little I had would fit in one tow sack. When Leroy left, I walked down to the Yellow Cab Company on the corner and got a cab to take me back to Mo'n's house. I sat in the back of that cab and felt like a woman. Mo'n said I became a woman when the red baron came, but I felt like a woman sitting in the back of that cab as Mrs. Leroy Washington. Not only was I now Leroy's wife, I was going to be a mama too. Leroy and I were going to start our own family, and our family would be filled with love.

I couldn't get back to the house fast enough to pack my things. I told Mo'n I was going to walk on around to Leroy's house. She wanted me to wait for him to get off because she thought I hadn't met his folks. Little did she know. I wasn't going to tell her that I had been over to Leroy's house and talked with his folks several times; the first being the day she went to the hospital to be with Daddy. I told her I didn't mind meeting them without Leroy. I was excited about getting to my new family. I didn't want to live in her house one more day. I said goodbye to Mo'n and David. I wasn't able to say bye to Sarah. God only knew where Sarah was; she had become a wild child. I left with a mile-wide smile on my face and walked over to Leroy's folks' house carrying everything I owned in a tan tow sack, and his baby inside of me. When I reached their house, I climbed the steps to the front door, excited and nervous at the same time. I knocked on the door and when the door opened I was greeted by both Ms. Ruth and Leroy Sr. They embraced and welcomed me in.

Leroy Sr. reached for my sack. "Let me take that for you baby."

"You straightened your hair out. It's right nice," Ms. Ruth commented.

"Thank you, I wish I had hair like yours," I said.

Taking my hand, she said, "Be careful what you ask for. All this hair is something to keep up. And God gave you the hair He wanted you to have, and He numbered every strand," she said, patting my hair. She was right, but what I've had to put up with the nappy hair on my head, I wouldn't wish it on my worst enemy. *Maybe I'll have a little girl and she will have hair like Leroy and Ms. Ruth.*

"Are you hungry?"

"No ma'am."

Leroy's mama and daddy were so nice to me, and I wondered if it would all change when they found out I was pregnant. I prayed silently that it wouldn't change and hoped God heard me because at that very moment, I promised Him that before I got too comfortable with my new family, in my new home, Leroy and I would tell Ms. Ruth and Leroy Sr. that I was pregnant. I didn't want to deceive them like I did Mo'n. I wanted to be honest with them, because they cared. I had drifted away in thought when Ms. Ruth offered to show me our room. She asked if I was okay and I told her I was.

"Well, let me show you your room." She walked me down a short, narrow hall to a room with a full-size bed, a night stand and a four-drawer dresser. It was decorated so beautiful for Leroy and me. There were two-panel curtains made of blue and white woven check; ruffles were sewn around each panel. The bedspread matched the curtains and was made from blue cheater cloth with a white background with blue and yellow cheater patterns. Ms. Ruth said she did all the sewing herself. It was the most beautiful room I had ever seen -- and large, too. Leroy told me later it was Ms. Ruth and Leroy Sr.'s room, but that they wanted us to have it. As I scanned the room, I was stunned when I saw, sitting in the corner, a white bassinet decorated in the same fabric as the curtains.

"You like it?" she asked. "We used it when Leroy was a baby, and Leroy Sr. put a fresh coat of paint on it." *So, you already know?* She must have seen the expression on my face because she walked over to me smiling and said, "Leroy told us." She knew already and she wasn't mad. Ms. Ruth said I looked tired and suggested I rest awhile. I was tired but it was two o'clock in the afternoon and at Mo'n's house you were hardly going to take a nap in the middle of the day. But I wasn't at Mo'n's; I was at home now, so I took Ms. Ruth up on her suggestion. The Washingtons' home was warm. I took that girdle off so the little one inside me could stretch out, and went to sleep. For the first time I dreamed; I dreamed sweet dreams.

Leroy stopped over at Mo'n's to get me when he got off, and she told him I had walked over already. When he got home I was sleeping, he thought, so he kissed me on my forehead and said, "Welcome home, Nadine," and walked out. I opened my eyes, with the biggest smile. *Here's to new beginnings.*

Chapter Eleven

Although I lived just across the field from Mo'n, I hardly went over to visit; when I did it was to see David. It wasn't long before Mo'n realized I was pregnant before I got married and every time I visited David, she talked down to me. It didn't matter to her that I was at least married to someone I really loved and that he was the father of the child I carried. But I was not heartbroken by anything she said, because she has never had anything nice to say to or about me -- so why would she change now?

When Big Sister found out I was married and out of the house, she came back for David, and Sarah went with them to Macon County. Mo'n now lived in that big house by herself. With David gone, I no longer had to deal with her negativity. I went months without seeing her, and it didn't bother me at all.

Our baby would be delivered at home by the neighborhood midwife, Ms. Fannie Mae, but I went to the community clinic regularly. The first time I went, I was already four months along so they gave me some big pink horse size pills to take. They said the pills were so I could have a healthy baby. The little baby inside me was growing. I was only five feet four inches in height, and one hundred five pounds. Carrying the baby, I got up to one hundred forty pounds. I was carrying a thirty-five pound baby and it wasn't going to be taken from a log; it was coming out of me. I remember what it felt like when Leroy put his thing in me for the first time, so I could only imagine what a thirty-five pound baby would feel like coming out of me. Oh, my God -- and I couldn't change my mind if I wanted to. The baby would be here soon and he or she was letting me know, because he was kicking me more and more. I was excited but I was scared too. Leroy said it was nothing to be scared about. That was easy for him to say, he ain't had a baby before. I talked to Ms. Ruth about me having a thirty-five pound baby and she told me the baby would not weigh thirty-five pounds. She said that was baby fat I had put on over the nine months and from the look of my stomach, the baby would probably weigh seven or eight pounds. That helped a little, but I couldn't understand how a seven- or eight-pound baby could come from me either.

I did not realize I had been pregnant almost nine months. That's a long time to carry something around on the inside of you; that's three months shy of a year, but such a short time for God to create a human being. *God, I thank you.* I asked Ms. Ruth about the pain and she told me it's different for everybody. She said the labor pains hurt for a while but as soon as the baby comes out, all the pain will go away. I felt a little better after talking to her. Mo'n had nine children, so I guess if it had been too bad she would have stopped after one -- but then, Daddy had the last word on that.

Most evenings after dinner, we settled down to watch the news. We liked watching Walter Cronkite because he always reported the news plain enough for everyone to understand. Leroy Sr. had left the table, but Leroy, Ms. Ruth, and I remained sitting at the table talking. We were about to get up and go up front when Leroy Sr. cried out, "Lord a mercy, Lord a mercy, y'all come in here." We all jumped up and rushed to the front of the house where we was not prepared to hear what Walter said next: "Good evening, Dr. Martin Luther King, the apostle of non-violence in the Civil Rights Movement, has been shot to death…"

We didn't hear anything after "shot to death" because we were hollering and crying like we had lost a loved one -- and we had. Ms. Ruth screamed, "Why, Lord? He didn't hurt nobody."

Leroy Sr. lost all the strength in his body and dropped to his knees. "He was a good man. He was a just man. All he wanted was justice for all." Neighbors started coming out their doors to see if other neighbors had heard the news. We gathered outside and cried together. In other cities, in protest, there had been killings, injuries, and lots of arrests, but not in Opelika.

We mourned Dr. King's death for days and on April 9th, we sat in front of our televisions and watched his funeral. What a sad day for black Americans. Dr. King's death shook the very foundation of what black Americans wanted as citizens of the United States. We didn't know if the movement would continue, but it wasn't long before we found out a friend of Dr. King, Ralph Abernathy, would fill his shoes. Ms. Ruth had a picture of Dr. King on her wall like the one Mo'n and Daddy had, and although Ralph Abernathy and others continued the fight, Ms. Ruth never took Dr. King's picture down. Dr. King's death disturbed me. I was restless for days after his death.

"Leroy, wake up -- I can't stop peeing. Leroy, wake up, something's wrong."

"What is it, Nadine?"

"I can't stop peeing."

I felt a pain and screamed. Ms. Ruth ran to our room with her housecoat half on. "Sounds like it's time -- Leroy, go down the street and tell Ms. Fannie Mae it's time." Before Leroy got back the pain was coming faster and I was just screaming. Leroy came back with Ms. Hot. I wondered what Ms. Hot was doing there. I thought he went to get Ms. Fannie Mae.

I screamed, "Lord Jesus, help me, Leroy, please hold me." He started toward me and Ms. Hot, aka Ms. Fannie Mae, warned him not to hold my hand a certain way or I might break it. She sent Ms. Ruth out to boil water and get some towels. By that time, I was hysterical, and she told Leroy he needed to leave the room because the baby was coming. I was hurting and scared to death. I wondered how many times already death had walked around my bed. They say when you are giving birth, death circles your bed, and the ninth time you die. The pains started coming so fast, I lost count and wondered how many times death had circled my bed because I felt like I was on my way to heaven anyhow.

Ms. Fannie Mae said, "Cut out all that noise and push. The sooner you push, the faster that baby gonna come out." I had a few choice words for her but I remembered death was circling my bed and didn't want to jinx myself by disrespecting my elder, so I pushed. To my surprise it did ease the pain. I pushed harder and heard a pop. "It's a boy." She spanked my baby and I heard him cry. At that moment for some reason I just started weeping uncontrollably. The tears came down as freely as when I could not stop peeing a few hours earlier but I felt no pain, just like Ms. Ruth told me.

Ms. Fannie Mae laid the baby on my stomach while I cried and she cut the umbilical cord. Leroy wanted to come in the room but she told him he had to wait until she cleaned me and the baby up. *I guess I beat death -- thank you, Jesus!* Ms. Fannie Mae cleaned the baby first, wrapped him in a towel, and took him to his daddy. She came back and asked if I was okay. I told her yes, but that I could use a nap. "After tonight, honey, you probably won't get much sleep for several months. The baby gonna want to fed on you right regular." Feed on me, what she mean, suck on my titties?

"We are going to feed him Carnation milk," I said.

"When you breastfeed, the baby don't get sick as much and they grow to be healthy," Ms. Fannie Mae said. *I guess I'm breastfeeding; I want my baby to be healthy.* Ms. Fannie Mae left me to rest while she cleaned the room. As soon as I drifted into a peaceful sleep, without warning, she pressed my stomach.

"Ouch, that shit hurt!" *Too late, I said it and couldn't take it back.* I had gone five months without saying a bad word. "I'm sorry, ma'am."

"That's quite all right -- that shit do hurt, but I have to make sure I get all the afterbirth out of you so it don't set up an infection and you die."

"I didn't know that."

Get all that shit out of me. Lord God please take all the filthy words from my lips. I didn't want my baby hearing or speaking that kind of language. Amen.

Our baby Rufus Lewis was born April 15, 1968 and he was perfect. The morning after R.L. was born, I was so hungry. Ms. Ruth took some peach preserve she had canned from the cabinet, made some hot butter biscuits and fried some streak-of-lean meat to go with it and brought me a big plate. The peaches were from Leroy's and my tree, and they tasted so good. I was so thankful for Ms. Ruth; she was nothing but good to me and treated me better than Mo'n ever treated me. As I took care of R.L., she took care of both of us.

For a while it was frustrating for R.L. and me because he didn't know how to latch on to my titties to feed. Mama Ruth showed me how to help him. God knows I wanted him to learn quickly because it was painful having all that milk stored up in my titties. The only thing good about milk being in my titties, was it made them look bigger.

Leroy went over to Mo'n's house to let her know about the baby. If it had been left up to me, she wouldn't know. Leroy didn't care for her either, but she was my mama and he respected that, so he walked over and told her the good news. She came over later that day and without asking, picked up my baby from his bassinet we had rolled into the living room.

"What you name him?"

"Rufus Lewis."

"Rufus?"

"Yes, after Ms. Ruth and Lewis, Daddy's middle name. We are going to call him R.L. like Daddy."

I could tell the name ticked Mo'n off. She was okay with Lewis, but naming him Rufus after Ms. Ruth didn't sit well with her at all. When I said "after Ms. Ruth," her facial expression changed. She looked like she had indigestion.

"Um huh," she murmured under her breath. "He looks just like you looked when you were born." *What have you been drinking? Little Rufus looked nothing like me and thank God for that!* My baby was beautiful. I had hair like barbed wire; his hair was just like his daddy's, black and curly. I was black; he was light-skinned and would be when he grew up, too. The color of the ears determines skin tone, and the backs of his ears were light, because I had already checked. Rufus would be light-skinned just like his daddy. After Mo'n told that lie, I was ready for her to leave. She almost caused me to start cussing again. She held Rufus for the longest five minutes and gave him back to me and left, but not soon enough. When she left I hoped that was her last visit. Ms. Ruth could see I was upset. When I placed Rufus back in his bassinet and pushed him back to Leroy's and my room, Ms. Ruth followed me. She couldn't get enough of Rufus either. She set on the bed and watched me tuck him in and when I was done, patted the bed and told me to sit next to her. She asked what had upset me so during Mo'n's visit.

"Mo'n was being hurtful when she said Rufus looked just like me when I was born."

"What was so hurtful about that, Nadine?"

"Ever since I can remember, Mo'n has called me black, ugly, and nappy head. So I know I'm ugly, but when I saw Rufus and how beautiful he was, I was so happy to know that in spite of my looks, I had a child that beautiful. And for Mo'n to compare him to me was her way of saying my baby was ugly like me."

"Nadine, you are not ugly. I guess you've heard that for so long, you've bought into it. But it's a lie straight from the pit of hell, you hear me? Honey child, I remember when Leroy first saw you, he ran home and told me he had seen a beautiful girl in the window." *The day I was in the window with no top on.* "He told me he was go-ing to marry you. I laughed and forgot all about that day until years later he came home and told me he got permission to court you. You should have seen him that Sunday; he was one happy young man. And the day you walked over here and sit on our front step, it didn't take me no time to see what Leroy saw in you. You had such a beautiful spirit and that made you so beautiful."

The sincerity in Ms. Ruth's voice, telling me I was beautiful, caused the hair on my arms to rise and my eyes to fill with tears. *No one had ever told me I was beautiful. Leroy told me he loved me but even he had never told me I was beautiful.* Ms. Ruth saw the tears flowing and she took me in her arms and held me as she talked to me. I laid my head in her bosom and wept. My mind went back to the day I watched from the window as Ms. Ruth came out the house, called Leroy to her, and gave him a big hug. Now, she was holding me, and her hug felt how I had imagined the day I watched her hug Leroy. *Please keep holding me*. I regressed to that young Nadine that just wanted a hug sometimes instead of a beating. I suddenly wanted to understand what I had done to deserve that kind of punishment. I had to have done something, because she didn't treat the others the way she treated me. Why didn't Mo'n tell me how to fix whatever it was I had done, so she could hold me close to her just once? I cried so much that day I felt like I was being cleansed. Cleansed from the self-hate I had embedded so deep in my soul over the years, as a result of Mo'n physical and emotional abuse.

"Cry, baby -- let it all out. It ain't about what's on the outside, anyway; it's what's on the inside, and how you love and treat others." Rubbing my hair she said, "So what if your hair is nappy, hair don't make you." I grieved that day for little Nadine and for little Rufus's mama. That day was the beginning of my freedom from the hurt that had me bound for years; and Ms. Ruth let me cry. She didn't force me to hold back the tears from the hurt I felt, like Mo'n did when she would beat me and threaten to give me more if I didn't dry up my tears. I heard Leroy walk in the room, but I never raised my head. I felt Ms. Ruth release one arm from around me, probably motioning for him to leave, because no one said a word and in a second, he was gone.

When I stopped crying, Ms. Ruth looked me in the eye and said, "Honey, beauty is in the eye of the beholder, and what I see in front of me is a beautiful young lady who loves my son, and who Leroy, Leroy Sr., and I love so very much." She gave me another squeeze and said, "God said we are fearfully and wonderfully made. You are beautiful, honey, and our little Rufus is one lucky baby to have you

for a mama -- and I'm one lucky mama to have you for a daughter."
Ms. Ruth gave me the motherly nurturing I needed, and it couldn't
have come at a better time. God knew I was thankful for her.

"So, don't let me hear you putting yourself down again. And
until you get that down in your spirit, I want you to wake up every
morning and say to yourself: I'm a beautiful, black woman."

"Thank you, Ms. Ruth -- I've never experienced motherly love,
and I love you too."

"And another thing -- you've called me Ms. Ruth long enough.
When am I gonna rate being called Mama Ruth?"

Of course I wanted to call her Mama Ruth; she was the sweetest
mama I ever knew. I thanked God for Mama Ruth.

Chapter Twelve

Mama Ruth wouldn't let me so much as look out the front door for three months after Rufus was born. I wasn't allowed to bathe, wash my hair, or cook for six months. She said my pores were open and I could get deadly sick if I took a full bath or washed my hair. She didn't allow me to cook, either. She said I was fresh and didn't need to be over the pots cooking.

Mo'n must have told Big Sister and Sarah about Rufus because a month or so later, she, Sarah and the boys came up for a visit. Big Sister brought R.L. lots of presents. She said I looked so happy and she was happy for me. She suggested we come to Macon County for Thanksgiving and Christmas dinner. In my excitement, I said okay, but Leroy quickly said, "We will be eating our first Thanksgiving and Christmas dinner together at home." My husband had spoken and I was in agreement with him, and we agreed we would visit each other sometime. We wrote to each other once in a while, but several Christmases passed before I talked to Big Sister again; our second child, Ezell was born. Leroy Sr. surprised us a few weeks before Christmas with a phone from Bell South. I wrote Big Sister and gave her our new phone number. She called at noon that Christmas to wish us a merry Christmas and it scared us because that was the first call we received since getting the telephone. It was good hearing from her; we talked for at least 30 minutes. She told me Sarah had married a police officer down in Macon County and he had brought her a beautiful home. She never mentioned Mo'n and neither did I. All I knew was she still lived over at the house alone. Esther had come down several times trying to get her to move back North with her, but Mo'n refused.

R.L. was just a fussing one Saturday afternoon and wanted to go out in the cold to play. We all had cabin fever from staying out of the cold and he really wanted to go out. Leroy was at work and Leroy Sr. was gone hunting and Mama Ruth told me I might as well dress him warm and take him out for a while and she would look after Ezell. As we played in the yard, something at Mo'n's house caught my eye. It looked like I saw fire in the window of Mo'n's bedroom. I walked closer toward the house to get a better view, and the curtains were on fire. I picked little R.L. up, took him in the house to Mama Ruth, and told her to call the fire station. I ran over to Mo'n's house, up the back steps, and beat on the door calling for her, but she didn't answer. I ran down the steps and around to the front, up all fifteen steps without getting tired, and beat on the front door and Mo'n still didn't answer. If she was unconscious in there, she could die, I thought. I was about to break out a window in the living room but I heard the fire truck and ran down the steps to wave to them. They pulled up and jumped out ready for action. I told them I believed my mama was in the house. One of the firemen climbed the steps two at a time and touched the front door. The fire had reached the living room, so they got a ladder and when through another window looking for Mo'n. The fire was spreading through the house like it was burning paper. Later we learned the wood Daddy used to build the house was old wood from the railroad. The wood had flammable fumes on it and should not have been reused. I'm sure his boss man knew this before he let Daddy take the wood.

Because of how fast the house was burning, they fought the fire from the ground and couldn't check for Mo'n until it was under control. I stood watching, hoping and praying Mo'n wasn't in the house. While the firemen were still putting out the fire, Mo'n rode up in a yellow cab. She jumped out of the cab carrying bags of vegetables she had bought downtown at the farmer's market. The watermelon man didn't come as often in the winter. She screamed, "My house, Lord a mercy, my house! R.L. built this house for me and it's all I got. Lord, please save my house."

The house couldn't be saved and it burned to the ground. Mo'n fainted and when I called her twice she didn't respond. Now was the perfect time for me to slap the shit out of her and bring her back around. Just as I drew back my hand, she opened her eyes and said, "Don't hit me, gal, I'm all right." She had lost everything. The only thing standing was the potbelly stove that kept us warm during the winter months, and a small metal box that Daddy had dared us to touch. He said it held all his important papers. Mo'n was relieved to see the box because the house insurance paper and all the other policies were in there. When the investigator asked Mo'n if she left anything on in the house when she left, she said no. I had noticed the gate to the stove where you put the wood had been left open but Mo'n swore she let the fire burn out before she left. I didn't believe her because she always kept that stove burning during the winter months. Mo'n had become such a liar over the years -- or was she always a liar?

Mo'n was temporarily homeless. Where was she going to stay now? She couldn't stay with me and I couldn't imagine her staying in Macon County with Big Sister after she let Daddy put her out in the street with nowhere to go, or with Sarah and her husband who Mo'n never wanted to meet because he never asked her for Sarah's hand in marriage. She didn't have any option but to go north, at least until the insurance paid off and she could build another house. For the time being, she stayed with Cousin Jessie Bell and Mr. Arthur Lee until Esther came down to get her.

Esther showed up two months later for Mo'n. Before they left, she came over with Mo'n to the house. I hadn't forgotten how she beat me in my head when Mo'n made her comb my hair. Every time I thought about how they treated me, I got depressed, but I didn't want to because I belonged to a good family now. But there was something about the two of them together that made me so uncomfortable, even with Leroy there to protect me. Esther came in the house like I was her favorite sister, and I knew that was a damn lie. In front of the Washingtons' she acted all high-falutin'. She gave me $10 to buy something for Rufus and Ezell, and I thanked her. She tried to touch the boys and they had a fit. They say children can see evil spirits on people. I guess they saw one on Esther.

I asked Mo'n how long it would be before the insurance paid the policy so she could rebuild. She said she didn't know, and she guessed they would be calling her. Was it just me, or was Mo'n sounding like she didn't care if the house was rebuilt or not? This was the same woman that about had a heart attack when she rode up to the house and saw it burning. Now all of a sudden "she guessed" they would be calling her? She gave birth and raised all nine of us in that house; my Daddy, her husband, built that house with his sweat and "she guessed" they would call her? It wasn't my house and I had nothing but bad memories, so I shouldn't care, but I did. It was the way she said it. I left the subject alone and saw them out to the porch. They said their goodbyes and walked to the car. Why

I thought they would embrace me, I don't know, but for some reason, I expected an embrace. Wrong family; the family that loved and embraced me was in the house. I waved goodbye and went back in the house. I felt a little sad, but it was not because I would miss them; I realized I had no kinfolks in Opelika now except my new family. Leroy knew I was a little sad and he embraced me and said now that he had a car, as soon as the weather warmed up, we would visit Big Sister. In the meantime, I had Leroy, our boys, Mama Ruth, and Leroy Sr. -- and we were a real family.

Chapter Thirteen

At the first sign of spring, the boys and I were out the door. Beautiful daffodils were beginning to bloom in Mama Ruth's flower bed. The air was so fresh and crisp this time of year and the trees were covered with blossoms. We walked around the house to see the pear, peach, and apricot trees. They were beautiful but Leroy's and my peach tree was a sight to see. Not only was it wide; it stood above all the other fruit trees. I stood admiring the trees as the March wind began to blow some of the blossoms off the trees. As the blossoms blew from the trees, it looked like it was snowing. Our boys had never seen snow because it rarely snows in Opelika. The last time it snowed I was fourteen, and the most snow we got was an inch. We would play in that inch of snow until it melted, which was almost as soon as it hit the ground. Although our boys had never seen real snow, they had read about it; we read to them a lot about everything. When they saw the blossoms falling, they ran around singing, "It's snowing, it's snowing." They were so smart, and Leroy and I were determined not to have it any other way.

While out in the yard I looked across the field at the ruins of what used to be Mo'n and Daddy's house. It remained the same as the day it burned to the ground. Enough time had passed for the insurance company to settle with Mo'n and for her to rebuild. I guess she had decided not to rebuild, and make her home up North.

Leroy kept his word about taking me to visit Big Sister. One Sunday morning, he loaded me and the boys in the car. Mama Ruth made us lunch to take with us so we wouldn't have to stop along the way. With so much injustice being done against black folks, Mama Ruth didn't trust the state trooper, or any of the other white officials for that matter. She stressed to Leroy that he should drive below the speed limit and not stop until we got to Big Sister's house. He promised her he would, because he was carrying precious cargo. I prayed nothing happened and that the trooper wouldn't pull us over. I knew if they did, they would have to kill Leroy before he allowed them to disrespect him in front of his family. We drove to Macon County and arrived at Big Sister's house without confrontation. Big Sister, Olivia, Larry, and David were glad to see us. We spent the first part of the day at Big Sister's house. I had hoped to see Sarah, her new house, and her husband while we were there. I was glad when she called and invited all of us over for dinner.

Big Sister was right; Sarah and her husband, Alfred, did indeed have a beautiful home. They had a concrete driveway and the yard was well-landscaped with hedge bushes in the front and on the side of the house. The living room made two of Mama Ruth and Leroy Sr.'s house, and she had three bedrooms, a den, kitchen, and two bathrooms! They had wall to wall carpeting throughout the house, and lots of cabinets and counter space with drawers. She even had a dishwasher and told me all she had to do was scrape the leftovers off the plates and put the dirty dishes in; push start, and leave it. They paid $12,200 for that house. Daddy's boss man had a nice house, but not like Sarah's. I raved so about their house until Leroy got up and walked outside.

I followed him and he said, "Sarah and Alfred can afford a nice house cause they just got a cat to feed."

"Leroy, I was just saying I like the house because I've never seen a house like this, that's all. You're a good provider and I'm happy with my life just the way it is. I swear."

"I know but I want to build you a house -- and I will, I promise you that."

"I know, Leroy, because you've never made me a promise you didn't keep."

I gave him a big hug and Sarah came to the door and said, "Love birds, it's time for dinner." Leroy and I held hands and went back in for dinner. Leroy told me as we traveled back to Opelika that Sarah's food was good, but her cooking couldn't touch mine. I loved it when he said nice things like that to me. And Sarah -- Alfred had sure tamed her; I could hardly believe she was the same Sarah. We enjoyed Big Sister, Sarah, and their family, but we had to get back up the highway before nightfall. That would be the beginning of us visiting regularly. Big Sister asked if R. L. and Ezell could spend summers with their cousins. We were so attached to the boys that we couldn't let them go for a whole summer, but we agreed to maybe a week or two when they got a little older.

On Ezell's second birthday, Mama Ruth baked a yellow cake with chocolate icing and Leroy picked up some ice milk on his way home from work. We had a few of the neighborhood children over and although Leroy had worked all day, he was outside with the children playing hide and seek. Leroy tried to find and tag the children before they ran back and touched the porch. The children had a ball and were full of energy, but I couldn't wait to walk them home and get back to the house and relax. Leroy washed up and I fixed his plate. The boys were still excited about the big red Flyer wagon

Ezell got for his birthday and they wanted their Daddy to take them back outside and pull them around in it. Leroy told them they had to wait until the next day to play with the wagon, but Mama Ruth told them they could ride it through the house if they were careful. They were her only grandchildren and she spoiled them rotten. R.L. helped Ezell in the wagon and pulled it into the kitchen where he kept pulling him around and around the kitchen table. Without me noticing him, Leroy went to the back where the boys were, and told them to bring me an envelope. When they came to the front in the wagon, I told them they needed to go back to the kitchen with the wagon, or I was going to put the wagon up.

"Mama, we have a present for you! Mama, we have a present for you!" They ignored my request and brought the envelope to me.

I had never been able to resist them, so I took the envelope and said to them, "Mama thanks you for her present -- now take the wagon back to the back."

R.L. looked at his Daddy and said, "Daddy, we gave Mama her present." He gave them a smile of approval and they turned the wagon around and went back to playing. When they were gone out of the room, I placed the envelope in my lap and went back to watching my favorite television show, *Julia*. Julia was played by a black woman. It was nice seeing a black woman in a lead role on television. She was beautiful too. I think her real name was Diahann Carroll. What a pretty name; even her hair was pretty. She was a nurse and she reminded me of Big Sister, dressed in a white uniform, white shoes, and white nurse hat. I imagined Big Sister wore the same uniform as Julia. I often thought of her working at the hospital in Macon County, helping people. Leroy got tired of waiting for me to open the envelope.

"Nadine, ain't you gonna open your present?"

"I've been playing with the boys all day, and play time is over." He just kept insisting that I open the envelope and to stop him from irritating me, I opened it. Reading it to myself, I said to him, "Okay, Leroy I opened it..."

I then realized what it was, and screamed. It was a loan approval letter for our house! I didn't even know Leroy was thinking about building yet. He said he wanted to surprise me and he did, on Ezell's birthday. I loved living with Mama Ruth and Leroy Sr.; I could have lived with them until I died, but I was happy that we would have our own home. Leroy wanted it too, and he had promised me he would build us a home. He told me when he saw how I carried on about Sarah's house; his goal was to make sure he got me a house to fuss over. I wasn't worried that he wouldn't get us a house, because he had yet to make me a promise he didn't keep. That's why I loved and appreciated him so much.

They started building on our house in 1970. It was a Jim Walters home and was being built on the property Leroy Sr. gave to Leroy. Our house sat between the ruins of the house I was raised in and Leroy's family home. Jim Walters Homes built houses for people who owned their land. Leroy didn't have to pay a penny for the house until we moved in. Our house was yellow and it had a living room, kitchen, one bathroom, and three bedrooms. The day we moved in was a happy day. We finally had our own place, and Mama Ruth and Leroy Sr. were within walking distance. I loved them so; they had been nothing but good to me from the first day I moved into their home.

Chapter Fourteen

Mo'n had settled in up North, and the land where the family home used to be remained vacant. Big Sister and Sarah could visit us now, but I found out they preferred we make the trip, which didn't sit too well with Leroy. He felt they thought they were too good to visit us, and he said we were not going to be running down there every time Big Sister called.

When R. L. turned ten and Ezell turned eight, we let them spend two weeks during the summer in Macon County. That gave me a chance to enjoy Big Sister and Sarah when we dropped the boys off and again when we went back to pick them up. They enjoyed it down there, playing and swimming with their cousins. It was also educational for them. They learned about the first black military pilots, The Tuskegee Airmen; Booker T. Washington who founded Tuskegee Institute; and George Washington Carver who created products from peanuts, sweet potatoes, and plants from the South. Big Sister lived just around the corner from the George Washington Carver Museum. The boys' summer visits continued up until Big Sister's boys started working during the summer to get ready to go off to college.

Big Sister and Albert were doing well by their children, making sure they got a good education. Albert and his siblings had gone to college. I guess his family was well to do; they had to be for all the children to go to college back in those days. *Lord, you don't reckon Big Sister married Albert for the money because he was old enough to be her daddy.* Albert was one year older than our daddy. And being with Albert, Big Sister got the opportunity to go to college and become a nurse. I wished I had been told about college. I was smart enough to go; I had earned two diplomas, one was just issued to Isaiah. College wasn't even mentioned in our house when I was growing up. You did good to graduate from high school, so it was good to see family furthering their education. College would be an option for our boys, too. Leroy said our boys were going to college if he had to work three jobs.

With the boys no longer visiting Big Sister and the children during the summer, I begged Leroy to take us to Macon County on Christmas Day. He didn't like the fact that we were always the ones traveling there, but he loved me and the boys and he always gave in to us after he finished cussing and fussing about it.

Big Sister gave Mo'n our phone number and she started calling to talk to R. L. and Ezell. They didn't really know her, but I told them she was their Grandma just like Mama Ruth, to help them understand better who they were talking to. But Mo'n was nothing like Mama Ruth and it didn't matter to them no way; they just enjoyed talking on the phone and hearing somebody talk back to them. She said she wanted to see us and asked if we would come for a visit. Leroy said he wasn't going, but if I wanted to go and take the boys he would be all right with that, and he would get us tickets to ride the Greyhound Bus. The thought of going there to see Mo'n and Esther upset my stomach so much, I told Leroy I couldn't do it. It brought back so many bad feelings; feelings I hadn't felt in a long time, so I knew I had to stay where I felt safe, and that was in

Opelika with Leroy. The next time Mo'n called I told her we would not be coming north, but she was welcome to come for a visit.

"You know I ain't staying in them there folks' house. When that sorry Leroy get man enough to put a roof over you and them churin's heads, I will come for a spell, but not before then."

What in the hell was she talking about? She pissed me off trying to insult my husband and I started to hang up. I didn't ask her to call us in the first place. *How in the hell you gonna call my husband lazy? Leroy's been working since he was a teenager. Your ass ain't worked a day in your life. We are doing fine and we're happy.* I took a deep breath.

"Mo'n, Leroy had us a house built; we live in our own home."

"He did? Well I'll be damned, when did he do that?"

"About five years ago, Mo'n."

My blood was boiling and I was ready to hang up on her. Her comments reminded me of why I didn't miss her nor cared to call her. We didn't need that negative energy of hers around our house anyway.

"Well, I reckon I'll have Esther get me a ticket and I'm gone try to come down in mid-August, if it's the Lord's will."

"Okay, Mo'n."

I hope it ain't His will, so you can stay your ass right where you're at. We hung up and I just screamed. Leroy just looked at me and said, "You want to torture yourself by having her visit -- that's on you, but she ain't gonna come up in my house acting like she own it; this is our house. And I ain't gonna stand for her disrespecting you either -- do she gonna hear a few choice words from me, and I'm gonna kick her out."

When August first came I was literally sick knowing Mo'n would be coming in a couple weeks. Leroy said if I was sick now, it would be worse when she arrived. He told me I was grown and I could call and tell her not to come. I wanted to but I didn't. I prayed that everything went well when she got to our home and that we would be cordial to each other; something she never was to me except on two occasions: when she told us Daddy had died, and the morning I was going to marry Leroy.

Hours after I prayed about Mo'n coming, I got a call from Esther that Mo'n was complaining about a stomach virus. She took her to the emergency room and her day in the hospital had turned into two weeks. She said the doctors didn't know what was wrong with her and that they were still running tests. I hated that she was in the hospital, but I couldn't help but think how the Lord works in mysterious ways; I prayed, and Mo'n wouldn't be coming to visit me for a while now, so I could be at ease again.

I prayed again for Mo'n. "Lord, I come before you for Mo'n; the doctors don't know what's wrong with her but you are the Doctor of doctors and you know. I ask you Lord, in the name of Jesus, to heal her like you did the woman in the Bible with the issue of blood; like you did the man at the pool of Bethesda; like you did when you caused the blind man to see and like you did when you healed the men with leprosy." *I don't know what leprosy is, Lord, but you healed the men.* "God, I know you're a healer because I've read it so many times in the Bible, so I know You can heal Mo'n if you want to because your word won't return void. I ask this in your precious son Jesus' name, amen."

When I finished, I just knew Mo'n would be all right. I felt so at peace until Esther called to tell me Mo'n had taken a turn for the worse, and the doctor was giving her 72 hours to live. *God, what is going on? I know you gave me the peace I felt after I finished praying for Mo'n. I know you gave me peace.* Esther said Mo'n was asking for me, and that if I could come, I needed to get there as soon as possible. Why was Mo'n asking to see me? I thought I would be the last of the children she wanted to see. Did she want to insult me one last time before she went to meet her Maker? *God, is this the reason why you gave me peace, so I could accept the fact that Mo'n was leaving this world? If so, I will get over that; I adjusted pretty well when my Daddy went on to glory, and I loved him.* I told Esther I had to talk to Leroy about me coming and she sighed like she had a problem with me saying that. She wanted to say more, but she held her peace. I wished she had said something. I wasn't that same nappy head child she once abused; I was going to cuss her out and call her everything but a child of God. I didn't owe her -- or Mo'n – anything, for that matter.

I asked Leroy if I should go and he told me to go. I called Big Sister down in Macon County and she told me she and Sarah was going to fly up the following day; flying was out of the question for me. I loved the song, "I'll Fly Away" but the song said "when I die hallelujah by and by" -- that's after I've died and my spirit's gone to be with the Lord, not while I'm still living. I packed a small suitcase and filled a brown paper bag with food and Leroy took me to the Greyhound Bus Station so we could check the bus schedule. It would take me two days to get there. Leroy felt I should fly.

"Leroy, I am not getting on no plane"

"Don't you want to get there while she's still alive?"

"They gave her three days; I will have one day to the good, if it's the Lord's will that I be there, but I'm not flying."

When we got to the bus station, the clerk told us a bus would be leaving in half an hour. Leroy got my ticket and gave me money for my trip back home and some to have in my pocketbook. Of course, I didn't keep it in my pocketbook -- I kept it in my bosom;

it was safe there. This would be my first time away from Leroy and the boys. The boys were upset and it upset me so, Leroy took them back to the house. We said our goodbyes and I promised the boys I would be back soon. As I waited to board the bus, I sat in the lobby and wished things had been better between Mo'n and me. I couldn't even cry for Mo'n the way I cried for Daddy or the way I cried the day Big Sister left home. The only emotions I felt at that moment were the result of leaving Leroy and the boys behind.

It took two days for me to get to Detroit. Isaiah picked me up at the bus station in the car my daddy left him. I was glad to see him because we'd always had a good relationship. It had a lot to do with us being the same age; all the other siblings except Sarah were much older than us. It also had to do with the fact that I was the reason he graduated from high school; I did all his homework. We greeted one another and he took my suitcase. I could tell he was doing well for himself. Isaiah's high school sweetheart, Charlestine, followed him to Detroit and they had one son and two daughters together. Charlestine loved her some Isaiah. In high school, she whipped many girls over him when she should have been whipping him. I could tell he really loved his children, and Charlestine too, but he was in no hurry to marry her and it seemed she was okay with that. En route to the hospital, I asked if there was any change with Mo'n and he said she seemed to be holding on. He told me Big Sister and Sarah had been there for two days.

When I walked in the hospital room they were all there: Big Sister, Sarah, Samuel, Solomon, Esther, Elijah, and Jeremiah all stood around the room. We greeted one another and when Mo'n heard my voice, in a frail voice she said, "Nadine, is that you?"

I looked over at the bed. "Yeah, Mo'n, it's me." She reached out her hand for me and I walked over to her bed and took hold of her hand. It felt so funny holding her hand; very awkward.

"I'se glad you made it. How my grandbabies?"

"They are fine, Mo'n."

"How you?"

"I'm fine, Mo'n."

"Good, cause they say I'm dying."

I told her I prayed for her and she did not respond. As if to change the subject, she called Esther to her bed and told them to go out a minute so she could talk to me alone. Why did they have to leave the room? What could she have to say to me that she didn't want them to hear? After they left the room, Mo'n said, "I know you think I been harder on you then the rest of them."

Why hell yeah, and you know it. The woman was on her deathbed so I lied. "No, ma'am."

The fragility in her voice left. "What I done told you bout lying? Sit down in that there chair, let me talk to you." Her voice sounded demonic and it scared me, but I sat down. "I need you to know the truth. I married your daddy when I was a young gal. He was years older than me and when I married him I ain't had nothing and they said I married up. I wanted to keep him happy and I did all I could to please R.L. I put him before me and my children. When Big Sister turned thirteen, R.L. always had her following him to the bootleggers' house. Folks talked about it but I just turned my head to it all because R. L. was the man of the house." I wondered why Mo'n was telling me this. She kept talking.

"When they left the house, they wouldn't return to the house until late when everybody was asleep. But I couldn't rest until everybody was in the house. I would just lay there. He always acted like he was too drunk to get to the bed and would have Sister help him to the study. The first time she went in to help him, I listened for her to come out and when she didn't I got up and went to the study door. I stood there at the door and listened to Ola Mae beg R.L. to get up off her."

"Mo'n, why are you telling me this? My daddy wouldn't do anything like that. You know I love my daddy -- why are you lying to me about my daddy?!"

"Gal, who you calling a liar?"

I wanted to say, "You!" but although I was grown and married with children, I didn't respond. Mo'n kept talking. "He would put his hand over her mouth, but I heard her crying because it hurt when he entered her privates, and I didn't say a word."

"Mo'n, what are you saying? Please stop!"

She ignored me. "That wasn't the last time your daddy fooled around with my child, and I didn't say nothing, I didn't say nothing." Mo'n was out of her mind -- Daddy did some shit, but that was his own child. He didn't mess with his child. He loved me and he never touched me the wrong way. Why was she lying? Daddy was dead now -- why was she lying! And why tell me? Had she told this to the others already? "Sister came up pregnant..." Now, she did get pregnant. I remembered that day and I remembered Daddy putting Big Sister out, but... "I knew it was R. L.'s child cause she hadn't fooled with nobody else."

Mo'n was so wrong. Big Sister came in late all the time -- she just didn't know it. A lot of times Big Sister would just be getting in when Mo'n made her get up and comb my hair. So, she was fooling around. But why was Mo'n telling me this about my daddy?

"Mo'n, I don't want to hear no more. Big Sister was fooling around. She came in late all the time. I know because we slept in the same bed."

"Listen to me, Nadine -- I knew the truth but I accused Big Sister of fooling around with some boy and when she started showing, I kept her in the house until she gave birth and I took you as my own."

She was delirious now; she was saying Big Sister was my mama. That wasn't possible because I was already born when Daddy put her out.

"Mo'n, you are my mama." *I wish you weren't, but you're my mama.*

"Nadine, you ain't my birth child."

"Mo'n, you're talking out your head. You are my mama. Let me get the nurse -- something is wrong, nurse!"

"Nadine, I know what I saying; I ain't your mama, Big Sister is."

"Mo'n, Big Sister is my sister. Nurse! Nurse!" The nurse ran in the room to check Mo'n and everybody but Big Sister followed her. "My Mo'n is talking out her head." I didn't realize she was in such bad condition. "Mo'n, you are going to be all right; I prayed for you." The nurse tried to take Mo'n's pulse and she snatched her wrist loose.

"Miss Lady, I'm fine, and I'm in my right mind, you hear? Now y'all leave me and Nadine alone. I need to talk to her."

I wanted to leave with the others, but I stayed.

"Nadine, before I die, I need you to know the truth."

She was starting to irritate me.

"I know the truth; you are my mama, so stop saying that. I remember the day Daddy put Big Sister out, we had just got in from school, Mo'n. I stood and watched her leave, Mo'n. Why are you doing this to me -- why are you trying to hurt me?"

"I wish to God it wasn't the truth -- but it is, Nadine. David is Big Sister's second child, you the first."

Before I realized what I was saying, I screamed, "Damn liar! You are a liar!" This was so crazy. How could Big Sister be my mama? If she was, she wouldn't have left me with Mo'n all those years knowing how she beat me unmerciful. If she was my mama, she would have come back as soon as she could to get me, but she moved to Macon County and started a family. Why was Mo'n lying? Over the years, she had become such a big liar, and she was lying now. I don't know what lie hurt the most, Mo'n saying Daddy fooled with his own child, or her saying Big Sister was my mama.

"R.L. was not Sister's father. I had her when I married R.L. and he loved her as his own until she became a teenager. After you were born, Sister never let him touch her again. She started running the streets and got pregnant again. That upset R.L. and he put her out in the street. I didn't even speak up for her."

"I remember that day. One of the few times you acted like you cared for me."

That was one of the worst days of my young life. I stood there in Mo'n hospital room, numb. I wanted to speak but no words would come out. I screamed, "For years, I wondered why you didn't love me and what I had done. I tried to do everything right; I bought home good grades and you still disliked me. As a young child, I tried to be invisible so I wouldn't make you mad -- and the more I tried, the worse you got. You tore down my self-esteem. You called me black, nappy head heifer like that was my name. You beat me naked like I was a slave. I have scars on me and inside of me that won't go away because of how you treated me. And now you lay there on your death bed and tell me you're sorry because you're dying. I died a long time ago. But I am alive again. I'm alive because I got a family that loves me. My children love me. I would never treat them the way you treated me. I'm sorry too, Mo'n -- I'm sorry I was ever born into this family."

When I walked toward the door to leave, Big Sister walked in. I looked at her in disgust. "Is it true what Mo'n said, you are my mama?" She didn't say anything. "Why didn't you tell me? Why did you leave me with her in hell? You knew how she treated me. Why didn't you come back and get me? Why did you go to Macon County and start your new life and forget all about me? What kind of mother would do that to her child? You left me there to live through hell. You wanted nothing to do with me until I got married -- then you wanted me and my family to visit so the cousins could play together and so I could see my niece and nephews. But in reality, the cousins are my sister and brothers, and my children's aunt and uncles."

I had to get out of that room. I felt my breath leaving me. I felt like I felt the first time Leroy laid on top of me, except I never got my breath back. I was suffocating. I needed to get out of that room; out of that state -- and I started to leave.

"Nadine, let me explain."

"You're a day late and a dollar short."

I ran out of that hospital room and Isaiah ran in. I guess he thought Mo'n had died. The others didn't run in the room. They knew what Mo'n had said to me. When Isaiah saw that Mo'n was still alive, he ran behind me.

"Are you okay? Where are you going?"

"Home to my family -- will you please go to your car and get my suitcase?"

"Why are you leaving now? Mo'n is dying!" *I hope she rests in peace.*

"Are you going to get my suitcase, or not?"

"Nadine, what's wrong?" I stood in front of the elevator and waited for the elevator door to open; Isaiah stood there with me. When the door opened, I got on and Isaiah followed.

"Nadine, please stay."

"I can't, I need to be with my family."

"We're your family."

It was obvious Isaiah didn't know about Big Sister being my mama. I didn't say another word because I didn't want to hurt him. When the elevator stopped on the first floor, I walked over to the front desk and asked if they would call me a cab. Isaiah offered to take me wherever I wanted to go, but I told him I wanted to be alone. He went to his car and got my suitcase and brought it to me. I thanked him and told him I would call him later, but I knew I would not be calling him any time soon. He told me he wished I would stay at least until I met my niece and nephews. I told him I just couldn't stay, but I would meet them another time. He wanted to talk like we did growing up, but I couldn't. He wanted to wait with me for the cab, but I insisted that he go back inside. He gave me a hug and went back inside the building.

While I waited outside for the cab, I walked over to a nearby telephone booth and made a collect call home to tell Leroy I was on my way home. By the time Leroy accepted my call, I was crying uncontrollably. He assumed Mo'n had died and asked why I didn't stay on for the funeral. I told him I needed to be with my real family and I would call when my bus got in. He told me he loved me and I said me too. He thought Mo'n had died, but it was me that felt like the zombie. When the cab dropped me off at the bus station, I had to wait three hours for the next bus. I had time to reflect on everything that had happened to me over the years. It became clear to me why Daddy's folks did not approve of Mo'n; she had a child already. Why Isaiah and I were the same age: Mo'n and Big Sister were pregnant at the same time by Daddy. I realized at that very moment, that every lick Mo'n gave me was to release the anger she had pent up on the inside because she allowed her husband to sleep with her daughter and didn't do anything about it, and I was the result of it. Why didn't she beat him? He was the guilty one, not me. Why did she stay, knowing Daddy had eyes for her child? Now, I knew why Esther mistreated me, hated combing my hair, and never offered me a ticket to come to Detroit. Now I understood why Daddy was so mad when the special meeting was for him. Deacon Jones had found out Daddy had messed with his child. Now I knew the reason Mo'n treated me different, but that didn't make it right. I was innocent.

When I got home, I told Leroy, Mama Ruth, and Leroy Sr. what had happened. Leroy said, "That's some messed up shit." Mama Ruth said it was rumored years earlier that Daddy was fooling with one of his gals, but she let it pass as just that, a rumor.

A week passed and I expected someone to call when Mo'n passed, but nobody called. It didn't matter to me anyway, because I was not going back to Detroit for the funeral.

Chapter Fifteen

Two weeks later, Isaiah called to say Mo'n was doing fine and would be released from the hospital in a couple of days. My mind immediately went back to the peace I had after praying for Mo'n and the words that dropped in my spirit that Mo'n sickness was not unto death. It appeared that after her confession, she miraculously recovered. I bet she wished she could take the confession back, but I'm glad it happened or I might never have known. All the older siblings knew I was Ola Mae's child, but they never said a word. Ola Mae knew what I was going through and had a chance to save me but she chose not to. It was more important to them to protect the Thomas name. Isaiah called from time to time, and I talked to him. When the others found out we talked, they started giving him messages to pass on to me. Esther started sending money for the boys and clothes for me. She put a note in the box that if I didn't want them, maybe I knew someone who could use them. I'm sure she thought she needed to say that because she thought I would throw them away. But she should have known I wasn't like her. They were good clothes, and all I couldn't wear, I gave to someone who could. Esther never said she was sorry but she tried to show me with things. I never thanked her for the money or boxes but she continued to send them periodically. I honestly believe they felt sorry for me but I didn't need their pity now; I needed them back when Mo'n was whipping my ass like it was going out of style.

Ola Mae called from Macon County every Saturday morning but I didn't speak with her. What was there to talk about -- how she abandoned me and went to Macon County and started a new life? I was an innocent child; I didn't ask to be born. Damn Big Sister, Mama, Ola Mae -- or whoever she was to me. She could keep enjoying the wonderful life she had in Macon County like she had done for years, and forget my damn number. She continued calling and writing, but I refused to talk to her. I put the letters she sent in one of the drawers on my china cabinet. Leroy told me I should talk to her and tell her to go to hell, kiss my ass or something, because he was tired of being the receptionist when she called. Ola Mae must have sent seven letters before she showed up at my door unannounced one Saturday morning; Leroy let her in. If I had known she was knocking, I would have let her knock like I did the Jehovah's Witnesses when they showed up every Saturday morning with their Watchtowers. I used to open the door and give them a donation for those little booklets and put them in the trash as soon as I closed my door, until I realized I was only helping them promote their beliefs. They don't believe that Jesus is The Way, The Truth, and The Life and that no man can get to Father God except through Jesus. I believe that, so I started pretending we were not home when they came knocking.

When I walked out from the back of the house to see who was at the door, Ola Mae was sitting on my sofa with a gray metal box in her lap. I recognized the box. It was Daddy's box, the one we were forbidden to touch; one of two items that survived the family house fire. What was Ola Mae doing with the box? When I walked in the room, Ola Mae stood up. "I don't expect you to forgive me or understand why I did what I did but I was young and scared too. Right after I got married, I called and told Mo'n I wanted to come and get you to live with me, and Daddy told me he would kill me if I ever showed up and tried to take you."

"When Daddy died, you could have got me."

"You were seventeen and I didn't think…"

"You could have tried! I lived in hell! But that's water under the bridge now. I have my own family and I don't need you now. I have boys that love me and a husband that saved me from your messed up family!"

There was nothing she could say. She passed the metal box to me.

"Mo'n wanted me to give this to you. When you open it, you will understand why."

"Leave it on the couch."

She put the box on the couch and started toward the door and stopped. When she turned back to face me, tears were running down her cheeks like water. "I didn't have anybody to go to for help and I didn't know what to do. I know saying I'm sorry is not enough and I wish I'd had the strength back then to do things differently, but I didn't. I'm going to give you time and I hope you let me back in your life on your terms; whether as your sister, mama, or just a friend."

She left and Leroy closed the door behind her. I sat on the sofa next to the box for what seemed like forever. Leroy came and sat next to me. "Nadine, ain't nothing in that box that can hurt you as bad as you been hurt already. If you don't want to open it, don't -- it's that simple. I'm here for you." I knew that was his way of trying to protect me from further hurt but it wasn't that simple; I needed to open the box.

When I opened the box, I expected to see my birth certificate inside that listed Ola Mae as my mama, but when I opened the box, the first thing I saw was the original deed to the house and the house insurance papers. Why did Mo'n send these to me? Why didn't she file the insurance claim so the family house could be rebuilt? I took the deed from the box and unfolded it. The house had been deeded to Nadine Thomas, me. Daddy had left the house to me. Mo'n discovered it when she opened the metal box to get the insurance papers. She had been in that box before when Daddy died, but she had no reason to look at the house information; all she needed was Daddy's burial policy. When she discovered that, she didn't care about the house being rebuilt. She put the deed and insurance papers back in the metal box and never told a soul. Rather than tell me Daddy left the house to me, she let the remnants of the house lie in ruins for years. She could have told me because despite all she had done to me, I had a conscience and would never have taken the house from her.

Daddy and Ola Mae were the two people I truly loved growing up, and to find out I was a product of Daddy and Ola Mae was too much to take in. Maybe it was a good thing I didn't find out about all the deception until after I was grown. I don't know if I would have been able to handle it as a child. I was already confused after Mo'n's confession, but to open that metal box and find out Daddy didn't leave anything to Mo'n changed my feelings for him. Even though Mo'n was low-down, she took good care of him. How could he die and leave the woman who took care of him and put him before her children, nothing? It wasn't that I felt sorry for Mo'n, because you reap what you sow and she never sowed me love. I just thought more of my Daddy and it turned out he wasn't who I thought he was. I was about to close the box when I saw a piece of masking tape, taped to the bottom of the box. When I pulled it up, there was a small key; on one side of the key were the numbers 5-2-2 and on the other side were the letters O-N-B. Mo'n must have been so upset about the house that she never saw the key. Leroy said it was a safe deposit box key and that ONB stood for Opelika National Bank. I never heard Daddy mention a safe deposit box. All his possessions were in the metal box, so I wasn't concerned about the key and set it aside. It wasn't a priority, so I told Leroy the next time I went to town I would stop by the bank and look in the box. One thing I knew for sure about Daddy was that he valued his possessions too much to leave them in a box where he couldn't reach them, or where the white man might be able to get to them.

Chapter Sixteen

My siblings and Mo'n continued to call from time to time and
I eventually spoke with them. They talked to me like nothing ever happened. Mo'n sounded so happy; I guess she was free
now that she had cleared her conscience. She always asked how we
were doing and wanted me to tell Leroy hello for her. Each time she
called, before she would hang up, she told me she loved me. Those
words coming from her were empty words. I just said bye and hung
up the telephone.

I submitted the insurance claim and was surprised they honored
it after all those years. I placed the money from the claim in a separate account until I decided how I wanted to use it. In 1982, I had
a house built on the family property and called it the Thomas family home. The house had a big family room, three bedrooms, two
baths, and a kitchen. I told Mo'n and the siblings about it and told
them it belonged to all of us and that when they came to visit, they
had a home to come to while they were in town. They even helped
me furnish it. It became a popular house and they came down regularly for class reunions, summer visits, and some Christmases. When
they were in town, I would go over to the house for short periods
of time; Leroy would come with me and then go back home. To
see them interact with me, you would have thought all was well and

forgotten. But years later, my soul still cried out for God to take that horrible pain away from my heart.

I had Leroy, my boys, Mama Ruth, and Leroy Sr., but I needed more. Even their love couldn't heal what was going on emotionally inside of me. My outer woman looked strong, but my insides cried out for help. I knew just a mere man or doctor could not fix what was going on inside of me. I needed the Doctor of all doctors – Jesus -- to do it.

Ever since I learned to read, I had read Daddy's Bible; not because I was saved, but because I loved to read, and there are some fascinating stories in the Bible. Over the years, I realized if you pray back to God His words, He can't do nothing but honor them because He is not a man that He should lie -- but I'd never had a personal relationship with Him. After everything I experienced over the last 27 years, I knew if I never needed the Lord before, I needed Him now. I started attending church more regularly; not the church Daddy, Mo'n, and the rest of us attended. We visited Mama Ruth's church, First Baptist, and it wasn't a church I could call my home church. First Baptist only sang from hymnals and they were too dignified to clap, lift their hands toward heaven, or say amen. When I went with Mama Ruth, she didn't tell me the rules, so when the choir started singing "At the Cross," I starting clapping and everybody except Mama Ruth turned and looked at me like I was possessed. After church, I asked Mama Ruth why she didn't tell me no clapping was allowed, and she told me folks can't tell you how to praise your God and you can't be moved by folks looking because your relationship with God is personal. She was right and I guess I was moved because I didn't have a personal relationship. Mama Ruth enjoyed the service but that was my first and last time going there.

A short time after visiting First Baptist with Mama Ruth, I passed a church named Peace Baptist on a street called Easy Street. God knows peace was what I needed. I needed a peace that surpassed all understanding because I was an emotional wreck. Leroy, the boys, and I started attending services at Peace Baptist. On our first visit, the opening hymn was "I'll Fly Away," and to me that was my sign from God that I was in the right place. They had a lot of activities going on during the week that I really enjoyed attending. Leroy didn't have a problem with me going so much; he said he could see a change in me since we started there. His only request was that I didn't expect him to go with me all the time. He said the relationship he had with God required that he visit God's house at eleven o'clock a.m., Sundays only, and I didn't try to force him to go more.

If it had not been for Leroy I don't know if I would have made it. I believe God sent him to the window that day to love me, and he loved me for me. Leroy was "God sent" even though he didn't think so. He said I was taking it too far when I said that, but I don't think I am. He said drinkers and smokers can't get into heaven; Leroy does love his beer and cigarettes, but for some reason I don't think that's going to keep him out of heaven. Leroy knows God; he's a good man and he takes care of his family like God requires. And if for no other reason, I think he will have at least one star in his crown up there because he loves me, nappy head and all.

I bought me another Bible just like the one Daddy had, and called it my healing Bible. I went from Genesis to Revelation highlighting every Scripture that mentioned healing. I read them over and over because I know God is a healer and He wanted to heal me. I knew in order for me to heal completely I had to forgive Mo'n, Ola Mae, and the rest of them -- but no matter how much I prayed,

I couldn't get past it. I had a pity party the other day and I struggled because I wanted to believe God for my healing and be this strong Christian, but the other part of me couldn't raise my hand in victory from the pain. When praying didn't help, I cleaned out the drawers to my china cabinet and came across the unopened letters Ola Mae had sent me years earlier, and read several of them. Reading them, I realized she was a victim too -- but the mother side of me, loving my boys so much that I'm willing to die for them, couldn't understand how a mother could leave her child knowing the abuse she would endure at the hands of her own mother. Reading the letters didn't help, and it caused me to replay the fact that when she started her new life in Macon County, she erased from her memories the fact that I was her daughter. The letters and praying weren't enough, and I found myself right back at square one. I didn't want to confide in anyone at the church because to look at me, I had it all together; I had even started teaching Sunday school.

I went to the man that has loved me since I was a young girl because I knew he wouldn't judge me; I knew he would be straight with me. Leroy said, "Baby, ain't nothing wrong with you going to see a head doctor."

I felt like he was saying I was crazy, and I was hurt because I never thought he would say something like that to me. He told me he knew I wasn't crazy, but that was some heavy shit to find out so many years later and that maybe a doctor could help me sort through it all. He told me, "You have the money -- use it and free yourself, you been in bondage long enough." Leroy reminded me that God works in mysterious way; that He is sovereign and He will use whatever He wants to use to heal you. He helped me to see that it's God that gave the doctors the skills to help His people.

Sure enough, I went to see a psychiatrist and I was able to sort through my emotions. It took some time, but I forgave Mo'n, Ola Mae, and the rest of them. I really did. I just haven't told them yet. While I was cleaning out the china cabinet drawers, I came across the key to the safe deposit box, which I had put there years earlier. I was in a cleaning mode so I took the key and went to the bank to clean out the box. That statement Mo'n made about Daddy's folks being some uppity niggers not having a pot to piss in, and if they had shit, she ain't seen none of it? I guess she hadn't seen any of it because Daddy had placed it all in the safe deposit box. Daddy left Mo'n something after all. I guess he was going to see if she would be smart enough to find it. He left her a substantial amount of money and each of his children too; even Ola Mae. My siblings and Mo'n continue to call from time to time, and I now hold long conversations with them. I haven't told them I forgave them yet, but eventually I will -- just like I will eventually tell them about the money.

What's the hurry? I went 27 years living a lie.

LaVergne, TN USA
02 December 2010
207007LV00004B/26/P